LIKE A CHARM

Also by Elle McNicoll

A Kind of Spark
Show Us Who You Are

LIKE A CHARM

ELLE McNICOLL

RANDOM HOUSE 🏠 NEW YORK

Text copyright © 2022 by Elle McNicoll
Jacket art copyright © 2023 by Sylvia Bi
Interior art used under license from Shutterstock

Visit us on the Web! rhcbooks.com

Educators and librarians, for a variety of teaching tools, visit us at RHTeachersLibrarians.com

Library of Congress Cataloging-in-Publication Data is available upon request.
ISBN 978-0-593-64913-8 (trade)—ISBN 978-0-593-64914-5 (lib. bdg.)—
ISBN 978-0-593-64915-2 (ebook)

The text of this book is set in 12.5-point Sabon LT Pro.
Interior design by Michelle Crowe

Printed in the United States of America
10 9 8 7 6 5 4 3 2 1
First Edition

To Ruby. To Evie. To Cy. To Minnie. To Fern. To Cara.
To the real Marley (told you I could make
him a boy). To Genevieve.

To all of the children who have read my books and
shown the world that girls like mine can be heroines.
You proved them all wrong, not me.

AUTHOR'S NOTE

The protagonist of this story has been diagnosed with dyspraxia, more formally known as developmental coordination disorder (DCD). It affects motor skills and processing. I was diagnosed at the age of nine. It makes my handwriting messy, but, like Ramya, no one has ever been allowed to tell me what I can or cannot do.

CHAPTER ONE

SEVEN YEARS AGO

The first time I ever saw one of them was the night that I saw my grandfather for the last time.

It was a foggy evening in Kensington, London. I was five and allowed to come downstairs to my parents' annual Christmas party, on the condition that I kept quiet and made myself useful by handing out the deviled eggs. I was the only person there my age; the adults towered over me like trees holding cocktail glasses.

I was invisible to them all. They laughed at things that weren't funny, and always laughed too loudly. Some would make cooing noises at me and tell me my dress was pretty. I didn't choose it, I thought it was ugly, but I said nothing.

Our house in London was narrow. High, but slender. People were crammed inside, and the presence of the guests stole every bit of air in the house. A mess of sound and smell and mystery to me. Seeing my parents and their friends outside the school playground, it was like entering a portal into another world. One of secret codes and a different language. One of false expressions. Sly glances and raised eyebrows. People would clink their glasses warmly, but their eyes were cool. Assessing.

Then I saw Grandpa. Like a fleck of gold underneath the dirt.

He was in the kitchen, washing his hands. I put my empty tray down on the table but ran toward him instead of picking up another.

"Ramya!"

At five, I was easy to lift up. I don't remember every word he ever said to me, but I can remember how they reached inside me and made everything better. I laughed as he swung me around.

"It's late for you to be up," he said, not sounding the least bit disapproving. "Spotted something new under the tree?"

I beamed. I knew he would bring presents.

"Where's Granny?"

"Home with a cold," he replied. "She didn't want to travel."

"Oh, okay."

"She picked out some of your presents, though."

"There's more than one?"

Mum and Dad disapproved of multiple presents, but Grandpa didn't think there was any other way.

I pulled on his dry hand, leaning my whole small body in the direction of the front room. Most people were through there, the largest room in the house. He let me move him down the hall to join the others.

"Oh!" I suddenly remembered. "My tray."

I hurried back into the kitchen, nodding to the hired member of staff as they handed me a new silver plate of food to give out. I concentrated very hard as I made my way back to the party, balancing the tray with care.

There was a crescendo of voices as I neared the room. I could hear Dad telling one of his work stories, over by the nine-foot Christmas tree. Mum was talking to some of her friends about how she didn't like the school I was going to. Grandpa sat by the grand piano, ignored by the rest of the room. One finger on the keys.

I joined him, placing my tray down on the lid of the shiny black instrument.

He smiled at me, our smile. The one that only I got. "Want to open a present early?"

I almost knocked the tray over in my excitement. "Yes!"

We both glanced over at Mum. Grandpa was her

father. He was every bit as soft as she was hard. Every part understanding, when she was quick to anger. Every bit warm, when she was . . .

He handed me a gift. A parcel wrapped in gold, with a pink satin ribbon.

"Granny wrapped it," he explained. "She's the master."

I laughed. Granny was dazzling and she liked everything to be beautiful and unique. I couldn't rip her paper; I opened the present with such care and thought. Knowing that the end result would be worth it.

And it was.

A soft woolen hat with a little nub in its middle. Baby pink, with red hearts. The material was so gentle; I noticed it was the same kind that my grandparents' sweaters were always made of.

"A hat!" I exclaimed, placing it on my head.

"A beret," he corrected, reaching over to tilt it slightly, so that it sat upon my long dark hair at an angle. "Your granny knows how smart you are. Now she wants you to be stylish."

I grinned. Only they ever told me that I was smart. Mum would get frustrated when I knocked things over, always muttering "Useless." Dad would just glance over, grimace, and then go back to his newspaper or his phone.

"I love it," I told Grandpa.

I turned with delight and vigor to grab my tray, only to stop dead. A tall woman with alabaster skin and a shimmering dress stood close to me. She grinned down at me, with teeth that were too white.

Every hair on my body stood on end. Every goose bump rose. It was like a thousand sewing needles were pressing against my skin.

"Play me a song?" she asked, her voice like wind chimes. Only it wasn't really a question at all. She wasn't asking.

I stared up at her.

Something flickered in her face. Like a ripple.

"Play me something," she repeated. A touch more weight in her voice.

I still could not move. I was frozen. I simply continued staring, feeling the urge to run.

Suddenly, Grandpa moved behind me. He settled himself upon the piano stool and began to play. As the music began, the woman settled. Her mouth turned up into a smile.

Then she opened her mouth. And sang.

I tore my eyes from her to look around the room. Everyone had stopped their conversation. Their gazes were all pinned to the woman, like a dog watching its master. She was singing a Christmas carol. In front of a fire, by a piano, to a room full of attentive listeners at a party. There was nothing unusual or untoward about any of it.

To them. To everyone else in the room. To me, something I couldn't name had happened. Something horrifying.

As she sang "O Come, O Come," her voice so pure and perfect, everyone seemed to move closer.

And I dropped my tray.

The sound of the silver crashing against the newly varnished floor was abrasive and shocking. Everyone started, including the woman. Grandpa stopped playing.

I glowered back at the woman. Defiantly.

The grin was completely gone from her face this time. She opened her mouth to say something when—

"Ramya!"

Mum appeared, pushing through the crowd. She grabbed my elbow.

"So sorry about that," she apologized to the woman profusely. "She's very clumsy. Way past her bedtime."

I thought about resisting as Mum began to walk me out of the room, but I was relieved to be going. I didn't want to be near that woman. I didn't want her in my house. I didn't want her near my family.

Mum marched me upstairs and into my room. She was angry, I could tell. She hauled open a drawer and pulled out some fresh pajamas before throwing them down on the bed.

"Get into these, brush your teeth, and then you're going to come down and apologize to Portia."

"No."

She glanced up in astonishment. "Excuse me?"

"No."

Dad appeared in the doorway, always the peacekeeper. He had heard the last part of the conversation.

"Come on, Rams," he said, his accent English. Not Scottish, like Mum's and Grandpa's. "Accidents happen, but you need to come and say good night."

"No." I repeated the word again. I had such a need to say it, more than ever before. It was instinctive. It was raw.

My parents were both completely flabbergasted. They gaped at each other in disbelief.

"I beg your pardon," Mum murmured, her voice dangerously quiet.

"Leave the girl be."

We all turned to see Grandpa. He had his coat and hat on, like he was ready to go home.

"Dad." Mum's voice was clipped and tight. "Go back downstairs. This is a family matter."

"Yes, and I'm family," Grandpa told her sternly. "Go back to your guests and stop snarling at the poor thing. She's too wee to be at one of your soirées anyway."

Mum obeyed him, shooting me one last glare as

Dad followed behind her. I could hear them muttering about my "sass" as they went back down to the party.

I suddenly felt the urge to cry.

"Now, now." Grandpa knelt in front of me and handed me a handkerchief from his woolen coat pocket. I examined it with a slightly trembling hand. It was white, with thistles embroidered on it. Each thistle had a letter. *J, I, L, C,* and *O.*

"James for me," he said, reading my mind. "Isabelle for your grandmother. Leanna for your mum's older sister."

"Cassandra for Mum," I said softly.

"Exactly so. And Opal for your youngest aunt."

My aunt. I had spoken to Aunt Leanna a couple of times over the phone. Her son was my age. She was bubbly and laughed a lot.

I had never met Aunt Opal.

"Your grandfather's favorite," Mum always said, perhaps a tad bitterly.

I wiped my eyes with the handkerchief and handed it back.

Grandpa regarded it for a moment. "Leanna sees the very best in people; your cousin is just like her. Your mother always sees the very worst. And your aunt Opal sees people for exactly what they are."

He looked around the room and a decision crossed his face.

"Ramya, what did you notice about that woman?"

My head shot up. I gawped at him. His face was completely serious, but his eyes were kind.

"Oh, yes," he said gently. "You noticed something, didn't you?"

"Noticed" was not the correct word, though. "I *felt* something."

"What did you feel?"

I was young then. I couldn't articulate what it was. I couldn't tell him that I just knew something was wrong the moment I heard her speak.

"I was scared."

He nodded. Listening to me. Taking me seriously. "But you didn't do what she wanted."

"What?"

"She asked you to play something. And you didn't."

I was confused. I tried to shake the confusion out of my head. "I don't understand."

"She asked you twice, and you didn't even think of doing it, did you?"

He wasn't telling me off. He was encouraging me. "No."

He barked out a laugh and hugged me. "Brave girl. Clever girl."

"I don't understand," I repeated.

"I know. I know you don't, pet. It's all okay. I want you to remember something: you belong at home. It's too easy to hide in this big city, too easy to vanish into the smoke."

"Home is here?"

"No, home is in Scotland. Someone with your gifts—"

"I don't have gifts," I said quietly, confused.

"It is a gift to look a command in the face and be able to tell the commander 'no.' Which is what you did tonight."

I wrinkled my nose. "I tell people 'no' all the time."

He positioned the beret once more, beaming at me in a way that made all my fears vanish. "Ramya, something is coming. Something is brewing, I can feel it every day as I walk in the street. Every time I turn on a television. Every time I open a newspaper. I feel it, and most people are too numb to notice. But not you. I knew it. You're special. You're just like—"

"So sorry to interrupt."

We both leaped to our feet. The strange woman stood in the doorway, her face serene but her eyes very sharp. Mum and Dad stood behind her.

"Portia has kindly come up to hear your apology, Ramya," Dad said pointedly. "So come on. Let's hear it."

To this day, I don't know what part of me told me to do it. But I stared directly at the woman and said, "I'm not sorry."

Portia's expression froze in place. Mum and Dad both made noises of horror. Mum strode into the room and grabbed me by the wrist.

"Apologize," she snapped, her mouth drawn tight and her eyes almost bulging in rage.

"No."

Portia let out a gasp. Dad closed his eyes.

"That's it," Mum snapped. "Get into bed. No privileges for you until next year, Ramya. Do you hear me?"

I nodded, never taking my eyes away from the tall woman in the doorway. She watched me right back. She seemed fascinated, as if I was something truly unexpected.

Mum barked at Grandpa to leave the room before he could say another word. They all made their way downstairs once more, Dad promising that this matter would be discussed in the morning. Portia was the last to leave and I was left alone in the dark.

I lay in bed for an hour, listening to the guests as their voices faded away. One by one, they left. I felt the door close each time. I could tell when Portia was leaving because I could hear Mum and Dad apologizing once more. Telling her that I was not normally this rude. That I was still learning how to be around people. That they were humiliated.

Then, once she was gone, the shouting began.

Mum was shouting. Grandpa was raising his

voice. Dad was wearily trying to calm everything down.

I slipped out of bed and scurried across the landing, sitting halfway down the stairs, my face pressed between two pillars beneath the banister.

"I told you not to bring those stupid tales into this house," Mum snapped. "I'm sick of hearing about your strange obsessions. You're not poisoning Ramya with it."

"Cass, she is lucky. You're lucky. Don't you see, she isn't like any of us."

"Yes, thank you for that, I'm well aware." Mum's voice was frenzied and exhausted. "We're being dragged into her Early Years class every other week to hear all about how unlike other people she is. Do you know she can't even hold a pen yet?"

I flinched.

"That's not important," Grandpa replied softly. "She's got something better than all of those other children. She's the reason we might actually have a fighting chance. Don't waste this child's life with silly ideas about 'normal,' when she has something—"

"Oh, Dad, shut up." Mum's voice was fragile, like she was about to cry. "Just stop. Get out. Get out and don't send cards. Don't call. Don't come around here anymore. I'm done. I'm through. I can't do this all over again. Get out and don't come back."

There was a horrible silence. I waited for Mum

to take it back immediately, to say she was sorry, but she didn't. There was a long pause. I wondered if they were each waiting to see if the other would back down, give in and say to forget the whole messy evening and that strange, hypnotic lady. But neither did. Mum let out a frustrated breath, her entire body radiating dismissal. Then Grandpa turned to go.

"No!" I screamed, running to the bottom of the stairs and launching myself at him. Holding on tight. "Don't leave."

"Get back upstairs," Mum said sharply. "Now."

I glared at her through tears and tightened my grip.

"It's okay, pet," Grandpa said quietly, pressing his rough hand against my ear. "It's all going to be fine."

I suddenly felt short of breath. As if my body had been hit by something sharp.

"Don't go."

"I have to, but only for now. It's a small sacrifice for the time being, but I'll see you again."

"No." Mum spoke softly. "For good."

I watched in stunned horror as Grandpa cast her one last glance before leaving. I had never seen any adult look so sad. I watched him walk out our heavy front door, as if I were watching a play. These had to be actors. Not my family, none of this could really be happening.

But it became too real when I heard the car start. When I could hear it driving away.

I ran. Out the front door and onto the black road. The only lights I could see now were the streetlamps. I felt my whole jaw shake and my lungs hurt as I watched the car turn the corner.

"Come back!" I yelled from the middle of the road. I didn't care about the other town houses. "Come back! Please!"

I started to sprint, trying to follow the car. But it was gone. Before I could even make it ten steps, he was gone.

"No," I howled. The despair that had descended upon our house was pulsing through me. "Don't leave me here!"

The night and our street were both too quiet. The only sound was me, crying.

"Get inside now," Dad barked from the stoop of our house. They meant business if he was the one shouting now.

I turned to go inside. And I saw her. Standing where Dad could not see, illuminated under a streetlamp.

That woman. Portia.

She smiled. A cruel, knowing smile.

My chest was heaving. With misery and now rage.

Then it started to rain. And she slipped away.

I stood alone in the middle of the road as the water came down. Rain landing on my face and mixing with the tears.

That was seven years ago now. It was the last time I ever saw my grandfather.

CHAPTER TWO

SEVEN YEARS ON

"Ramya? Ramya!"

My eyes are closed. I can hear my name being called. But I'm inside my own memory. Remembering that dark road and the car. And *her*.

"Ramya Knox, come down from there, this minute!"

My eyes shoot open.

I'm not five years old anymore. I'm not in London anymore. I'm barely even that girl anymore.

Instead, I'm in Edinburgh. At my new school. Sitting on top of the bike shed.

"Hello, Mr. Ishmael," I call down, smiling innocently. "I'm just eating my lunch."

Mr. Ishmael, my Head of Year, squints up at

me in terror. He's a younger teacher. The kind who makes decent jokes and knows about the latest internet drama. He isn't laughing now, though; he looks horrified.

"Come down before you break your neck!"

I snort, swinging my legs as they dangle over the edge of the flat roof. "It's only five feet high, Mr. Ishmael."

"Nevertheless. Come. Down."

I shove the last piece of my sandwich into my mouth. "I'm allowed to eat lunch, sir."

"Yes. On the ground. And you've had more than enough time. Hop off, we're late."

No "we" about it. He means me. *I'm* late. Except I'm not. I had no intention of going at all.

"Ramya." His voice is soft now. Empathetic. It grates on me. "We can talk all about it. But you need to get down, pal."

I swallow my bite, then use my hands to launch myself onto the playground. I bend my knees when I land, and I can hear his breath catch.

"Thank you," he says, releasing a sigh. He starts to escort me across the playground, toward the main building.

"Let's have a quick chat before you head to Mrs. Burns."

I roll my eyes but follow him down the winding school corridor toward his office. This is not just a new school for me, it's also senior school. It's gray. It's metallic. The walls and floors are all designed so that any mess can be wiped clean instantly. There is hardly any color. No artwork on the walls. Instead, there are lockers and trophy cabinets.

We reach his office, and he opens the door for me. I saunter inside and collapse into the chair opposite his.

I'm very familiar with the inside of Mr. Ishmael's office. It's only been a couple of months since I started.

"All right," he says, settling across from me. "What's going on?"

I drum my fingers against the armrests of the chair. "Nothing."

"Ramya." His voice is gratingly understanding. "You know you're late for your workshop. You skipped last week's altogether."

I sniff. So they did notice.

"I didn't feel like it today."

"Uh-huh."

"Hey, I'm not sure what the purpose of getting me to write the same thing over and over is, exactly."

"The occupational therapist said you need to practice with the tools she recommended."

"My hand hurts and it's boring. And why do I have to miss my whole lunch break once a week because I'm dyspraxic, while the G and T kids get to go to their workshops during lessons?"

Gifted and Talented. An insufferable, smug bunch.

"You could be in G and T, Ramya," Mr. Ishmael says tiredly. "Easily. You're one of the smartest students I've seen in some time."

He's examining his glasses as he wipes the lenses clean. I'm glad; I don't want him looking at me. I don't want him to see my reaction to that admission.

"I don't like those workshops, Mr. Ishmael," I say honestly. "I don't like how they make me feel. They make me feel . . ."

Less than. Different.

"The lessons are to help you get better with your motor skills," he says gently. "To get that hand-writing a bit neater. To help with public speaking. Though, to be fair, you don't need a lot of improvement in that regard. But your written work needs some improvement."

I meet his gaze with defiance. "Everyone uses computers once they leave school."

"I've done my homework on you," he says, smiling broadly. "You were a champion swimmer at your old school."

"Yes," I reply flatly. "It had a swimming pool."

I had to work twice as hard to master the strokes, but once I had them down, I could outperform anyone.

"But your teachers said you got quieter and quieter as elementary school went on."

"Hmm," I muse. "Could that have something to do with the fact that teachers are always telling us to shut up?"

"Don't say 'shut up,' please."

I glare. "I was in the debating club. Did they tell you that?"

I was. Before I was asked to leave. The word "merciless" was bandied about in regard to my rebuttal.

I've never been overly social. Go to school. Head down. Ignore whatever drama is going on. Go straight home. Do homework. Watch films. Go to bed.

I don't like people. I don't like company that isn't my own. It baffles me; why does this school find that so troubling? I'm not spraying graffiti on the walls or ripping pages out of library books. So I wish they would leave me alone.

Edinburgh is a city but it is not a city like London. In London, you're encouraged to mind your own business. Mum and Dad were always good about keeping my interactions with other people to a minimum, but that's harder for them now that we live in Scotland. It's much friendlier here. People ask you questions and remember your name.

Also, now that my parents have found their dream job together, I'm expected to be much more independent. Scooting to and from school, no matter the weather.

It's small for a city. More like a really big village.

I turn back to Mr. Ishmael, who is taking a sip of water.

"We just know that some extra support with this transition won't go amiss. You're in a few beginner groups at the moment, but I know you can move up, Ramya. I know it. I don't know why you hide your ability, but we can help you get there. We've got some great new staff members joining us this term. One's a baroness."

"Whoopee."

"She's worked with a lot of Special Educational Needs departments before. She might have some great insights."

He doesn't get it. He thinks it's about motivation. About believing in myself. He doesn't understand that it would take an entire rewiring and restructuring of the way this school is run for me to actually feel supported. I know I'm made fine. They just need a bit of time to realize that as well.

"Having a learning difficulty is nothing to be ashamed of," he says agreeably.

I bite the inside of my cheek. "I know that."

"Lots of brilliant people had to face challenges when they were your age."

If he talks about Einstein being dyslexic, I won't be responsible for my actions. He's a good teacher. One of the best I've had. He genuinely cares, I can tell by the dark circles under his eyes and because he always rubs his neck. He stays late to grade work and check on the after-school club. He's usually the first one here and the last to leave.

But he doesn't know what this outside-looking-in state of being feels like. To remember a million facts but find it hard to concentrate on the boring ones they want you to recite. To know a faster way of solving the problem that the teacher is describing, only to then be told you're not "doing it properly."

Not to mention the absolute humiliation ritual that is PE.

"Can I take you along to Mrs. Burns, then?" he asks softly.

My shoulders drop. It's not a battle I feel like fighting today.

"Yes," I murmur.

We move through the corridors, where the other students are screeching and hooting. The sound of people's bodies slamming excitedly into lockers is an irritant. Lucy and her gang are all sitting against the radiators, surveying their savanna and watching for the school hallway equivalent of a particularly vulnerable gazelle.

It will never be me. I've been there. Been the gazelle of the school hallway, back in London. If anyone tries it here, they'll get a kick. The kind that incapacitates a lion and sends a message to its pride.

I convey this exact thought through a vibe I can give off at will. Lucy sees it and gives an almost imperceptible nod.

She knows not to bother me. Everyone does. I don't bother them and they'll regret it if they bother me. Lucy and her gang have a few victims they like to torment, and I stay out of it.

I'm not about saving people. No one tried to save me, after all.

The air feels meaner these days. I can't explain it. I don't particularly care to. A few bullies have taken things too far. A few children have moved to another school. There is somehow a nastiness creeping around, like a gas you cannot smell.

We reach Mrs. Burns's room and Mr. Ishmael puts on a massive grin.

"Afternoon, Mrs. Burns. Got a latecomer here for you."

The other members of the workshop are all seated around a table, and they glance up in surprise at our arrival. Mrs. Burns is slightly nervous.

"Oh, Ramya," she says faintly. "Good. Come in, then."

I slump into the only available chair and stare at the others.

All boys.

I feel a twinge of shame. No other girl's handwriting is considered as messy as mine. I know I shouldn't care; I know it's not important, but it needles at me.

"All right, Ramya, here's your practice book," Mrs. Burns says, sliding a workbook over to me. I flip it open, defeated. It's similar to what the occupational therapist made me do in the hospital. Lots of writing and "draw this shape as accurately as you can."

I glance longingly at the clock on the wall.

Mrs. Burns sips from a tepid-looking glass of water while we work in silence. Each time I press the pen to paper, I feel a pinch of frustration. This is boring. This is dull. This is sucking something out of me, something that I can't name.

School feels like climbing up a really steep hill. Each time I reach to grab a patch of crag or a rock, desperate to haul myself farther up, someone appears to tell me that I'm doing it wrong. They don't help or offer a suggestion; they simply tell me that I'll never make it to the top of the hill if I carry on like that. The more I push and climb, the more I struggle and grasp and gasp, the more disapproving the faces become.

It makes me want to let go. I might as well fall to the bottom of the mountain rather than keep climbing. I sometimes think they don't want me to reach the top.

I loved the idea of school once. Getting all my stationery together in a new bag. A homework agenda. Colorful highlighters. Putting an ordered pencil case together to face a new year.

The novelty wore off when they all hated how I held those pens. How I wrote on the paper.

"Ramya," Mrs. Burns stage-whispers at me from across the table. "I think your hat is lovely but it's not uniform, sweets."

She's not being unkind. She's only doing her job. But I clench my jaw. I don't touch my beret.

"Ramya," she repeats gently. "Let's take off the hat, please."

I press my pen down so heavily, it creates a dark crater of ink on the workbook.

Suddenly, Mrs. Burns's glass of water shatters.

She shrieks and we all jump. I stare at the fractured mess of glass, and the water that has spilled all over the table.

"Goodness," Mrs. Burns breathes, fanning herself with her undone sleeve. "Gave myself a real fright there. Frankie, can you grab me a paper towel, please?"

Frankie jumps to obey, but I keep staring at the glass.

She wasn't holding it when it broke. I know she wasn't.

We move our workbooks as Mrs. Burns accepts a cloth from Frankie and begins to clean up the mess. I'm about to remove my beret as a peace offering when a sharp knock on the door interrupts us.

"Now what?" sighs Mrs. Burns before calling in a louder voice, "Come in!"

A nervous sixth grader pokes their head through the door. "Is Ramya Knox in here, miss?"

Mrs. Burns gestures to me, and I nod. "That's me."

"They need you to come to the office," the sixth grader says, avoiding my gaze.

"Okay," I say slowly. I move to leave the room, but he nods toward my bag.

"You won't be coming back."

He doesn't say it in an ominous way. He says it carefully. But it sends tremors through me and dries up my throat. I snatch my bag and fix my beret on my head, leaving the Special Educational Needs Department room without a backward glance.

I go over every negative scenario in my head as I walk to the office, in the reception area of the school. Expulsion? For sitting on the roof of the bike shed? For refusing to take off my beret?

However, as I reach the front desk, all of that flies out of my mind. I can taste the tension in the room.

My eyes shoot to the large fish tank over by the seating area.

Where I notice a boy in my year. He's sitting on the guest sofa with his head between his legs.

Marley. My cousin.

I look to Mrs. Hudson, the receptionist. She's staring at me with an expression that makes me want to turn and run away.

"What is it?" I say, almost inaudibly. "What's wrong?"

"Ramya." She leans close to me, and I want to snatch the landline out of her hands and hurl it against the wall. "Your aunt Leanna has called us to say you and Marley need to be sent home."

I'm biting my lip so hard; it's going to bleed. "Why?"

Her eyes are wide, and I can tell without ever having spoken to her before that she hates giving bad news. That it's not something she's ever anticipated having to do in this job.

"Your grandfather passed away."

By the time she says the third word, my head is all the way down and I'm trying to focus on the floor. It's blurry. Blue carpet. With tiny ridges. I can feel someone touching me, saying soothing words, but I don't know what they are.

"Go and sit with Marley until your family gets

here," Mrs. Hudson says, physically steering me toward the large blue sofa that's for visitors.

I fall down next to my doubled-over cousin and stare ahead.

Mrs. Hudson is speaking hurriedly on the phone to someone. Another member of the support staff jogs in and grabs a Post-it note from her. She throws us an expression of pity before jogging out again.

There is a moment of awareness. When I fully recognize that the person beside me is family. The boy holding a comic book with some superhero I don't recognize on the cover.

But we've never spoken before. So we don't start now.

CHAPTER THREE

BLACK BERET

My going to the funeral started a massive argument. Mum initially forbade it. She said I was too young. That funeral services aren't for children and that I hardly knew him anyway. That made me scream. Then she screamed. Then Dad stepped in and told us both to calm down, and so we both screamed at him. For behaving as though being calm is somehow the right thing to do at a time like this.

I ended up begging. So Mum relented. She said she couldn't go. She wouldn't. But she would drop me off.

"How is she getting home?" Dad asks as we pull up to the cemetery.

It's a Saturday in October. The place is ready to turn to tawny. It's peaceful.

"I've got my bus pass," I answer before Mum can speak. "I'm getting the forty-five to town and then walking."

We live in the New Town. It's pretty old, to be fair. But not as old as the Old Town, which is ancient and right beneath the castle.

It doesn't take too long to learn this city.

"Fine," Mum says, sniffing and putting the hand brake on. "Do you need money?"

"No," I say curtly. "See you later."

I can feel their eyes on me as I walk down the small mound before joining the path toward the building. I don't know what to call it.

I can hear gentle organ music as I approach, and someone is standing at the door. Someone I don't recognize.

I turn around and watch Mum and Dad pull off and drive away. They didn't even stay to see me go in.

I think the person at the door is the funeral director. He's holding programs.

"Are you family?" he asks delicately.

I don't know why I hesitate for so long. But I eventually nod. "Yes."

"You can sit in one of the pews at the front," he

tells me, handing me a program. A crisp beige card with gold foil print. I move down the aisle of the building and sit in the front row. There is currently no other family here. A few elderly people peppered in the pews behind me, all reading their programs, very soberly.

I can feel them enter the room before I actually see them.

I stare ahead for a moment, listening to the sound of heels on the funeral chapel floor. Then I turn.

My grandmother. Isabelle Stewart-Napier. She's tall and willowy, with long silver hair. It sits smoothly over her right shoulder. A pearl choker, a smartly fitted black jacket, and a matching skirt. She has her arm around my aunt Leanna. Not so tall. Not as lean. But warm, with sunny yellow hair. Her face is red and splotchy from tears.

Marley is on Aunt Leanna's other side. In a smart black suit.

None of them have noticed me as they move to sit in the front pew on the other side of the aisle. Gran is whispering to a distressed Aunt Leanna. Marley is fidgeting with his buttons.

The service is about to start when a man, a touch younger than Mum and Dad, jogs down the aisle and slides in next to Marley and Aunt Leanna. He's wearing a nice suit, and he appears to be worried about my aunt and cousin. He kisses Marley on the head and then Leanna on the cheek. He presses a quick kiss on her hand and squeezes it tight.

He must be Aunt Leanna's new partner.

"Thank you." A minister takes to the platform to speak as the organ music fades out. "Welcome. We are here today to honor the memory of a remarkable man. A beloved husband, father, and grandfather. James Stewart-Napier."

I'm glad I'm alone in my pew. There's no one to see my shoulders tremble. No one to catch the quiet sounds I'm making.

When the coffin is brought in, I muster up the courage to turn and acknowledge it.

And I freeze. Standing at the back of the room are two strange figures. The first, a man I've never seen. Not even in photographs. Young, clean-shaven, and wearing a pin-striped suit. He catches me looking, so I rip my eyes away.

The other is a woman who must be in her twenties. Hair piled high on her head. Dark clothes and dark glasses. Everything about her is dark, apart from the gloves she's wearing. They're bright turquoise. And they only cover her fingers; they don't stretch all the way to the wrist. They stand out brightly against her somber clothing.

My aunt Opal. Grandpa's favorite.

I STAY HIDDEN IN THE far end of my pew, concealed from the overhead lighting as people start filing out of the room. I watch my cousin, aunt, and grandmother leave. Along with Leanna's partner. He's checking in on all three of them as they move, making sure they're all right.

By the time I start to leave, the man who was standing next to Aunt Opal is the only one left. To my astonishment, he beams widely at me. As if we're at a family reunion, rather than a funeral.

"Ramya."

I tell myself not to be unnerved. This is not a random gathering, and it's not a secret that he was my grandfather.

"Yes."

He holds out his hand and, in a swift and sudden movement, a small business card appears. I blink, annoyed with myself for missing the sleight of hand. I take the card. It's red with black print.

"Avizandum?" I say, turning it over and then glaring at him. "What's that?"

"Many things. It's a term in Scottish law." He wears a catlike smile. "I'm a lawyer. Of sorts."

"I'm not supposed to talk to strangers," I tell him shortly. "Especially lawyers."

"The address on the other side." He gestures to the card. "It's a bookshop. On Candlemaker Row. My offices are above the shop, but that's by the by."

"Cool," I say sarcastically. "This is how kids end up on the news. So I'll be seeing you."

I walk by him and start heading in the same direction as the rest of the party, who are moving toward the building for the reception.

"Your grandfather left you something."

I stop. It's probably the only thing this stranger could have said to catch my interest. Suspicion and spiky hope pulse in my ears.

I turn. The stranger has donned some small, round shaded spectacles to protect his knowing eyes from the autumn sunshine. He grins.

"What?" I ask quietly.

"He left most things of value to your aunt, cousin, and grandmother, to be certain. All his capital and property, so don't get excited about a manor in the Highlands or that shop in the Grassmarket."

He's referring to my grandmother's house by Loch Ness, and the flat Aunt Leanna and Marley live in. Above their shop in town. It sells things like stones and odd curiosities. Dad has often lamented the fact that Aunt Leanna is "squandering prime real estate in a tourist hot spot."

"You're not a lawyer," I say carefully, never taking my eyes from him.

"I am, of sorts," he replies cheerfully. "I help people transition and manage their affairs."

I want so desperately to ask what my grandfather left me. But I don't want to give him the satisfaction. We stare at each other. His lips are twisted strangely, thin like a newly cut piece of twine.

"Come to that address after you've paid your respects, and I'll show you," he instructs, turning to walk away.

I'm about to fire back that I'm not prepared to be kidnapped when he calls one last remark over his shoulder as he leaves the courtyard.

"Your aunt Leanna's shop is only around the corner from Avizandum."

He's right. Candlemaker Row winds down into the open square where Leanna's shop is situated.

"Perfectly safe," I hear him add.

I round on him, but he's vanished. I glance around my green surroundings and over to the reception building, where I can see everyone gathering around a large buffet table.

No sign of him.

I do see Aunt Opal up on the hill. Her gloves stand out against everything else she's wearing. A taxi pulls up and she gets inside. I watch it pull away, all the while wondering if she'll glance out the window and spot me.

She does not.

I cast an image of Mum and her two sisters in my mind. None of them are easy for me to understand. Mum, who treats her job like it's another child. Aunt Leanna, who laughs and cries so easily, and changes her appearance with every season.

And then Opal. All I know about her is that she's the youngest and was Grandpa's favorite.

I make my way into the reception, thinking about the stranger's mysterious offer. I'm still holding the business card. I slip it into the shallow pocket of the black dress I'm wearing.

Then I bump into the buffet table, my clumsiness almost sending a platter of food to the floor.

A hand catches it, steadying me at the same time.

"Silly place to put a table."

I glance up into a new face. Aunt Leanna's partner. He is every bit as friendly as the stranger was unnerving. He is both sympathetic and cheerful.

"You must be Ramya. I'm Ren."

"I know," I say distractedly, gesturing toward Leanna. She's on the other side of the room, shaking hands with people. "You're with my aunt Leanna."

"And Marley," he adds. "He says you go to the same school?"

"Yeah. We're not in the same classes, though. He's advanced group."

"He's very smart," Ren acknowledges, with affection. Then his eyebrows draw together in concern. "How are you coping? You doing all right?"

I feel pushed off-balance at the compassion in his voice, but I stiffen my spine. "I'm fine."

He smiles softly and then glances around. "Aren't your mother and father here?"

I can hear the note of surprise in his voice. I know it must seem odd for me to be here alone. But if they knew how angry, even frightened, Mum seemed at the idea of coming . . . I can't explain years of family history when I don't even understand it myself.

"They work a lot," I say impassively. "They're news anchors."

He is impressed. People usually are. They're used to hearing about parents who work in an office filing taxes or selling things over the phone. Not parents who sit on a sofa in front of television cameras, discussing the daily headlines.

"That's exciting," he says. "Still, I'm sorry you had to come here alone. It must have been really difficult."

It was. It was very difficult. Sitting alone on that pew, feeling like I had some kind of invisibility fog over me, was difficult. Everything about today and the last couple of months has been difficult.

Which is why I begrudgingly appreciate Ren for being decent.

"Have you eaten?" he asks gingerly, casting an eye over the generous buffet table that we're both standing next to. "I know James would have approved of all this."

I glance up. "You knew Grandpa?"

He wears the kind of smile that gets passed around a lot during funerals. "Only a bit. Leanna introduced us shortly before he fell really ill."

I have a hive of questions inside me. Stinging me. "They didn't tell me he was unwell."

The same sad expression. "They probably didn't want to worry you."

Someone calls his name from across the room, but instead of abandoning me straightaway, he squeezes my shoulder and says, "I'm so very sorry, Ramya."

I watch him go. Feeling the lasting impression of the squeeze. He joins Leanna, Marley, and some other people and I experience a pang of pain. It's never fun to be left out in general, but being left out at your own grandfather's funeral is something else entirely.

I catch my cousin's eye for a moment and look away sharply. He was laughing at something Ren said. Even Aunt Leanna seems cheered by his words. Her mascara is wet and dewy under her eyes but she's laughing now.

I jump as someone appears next to me, carrying an empty plate and a pair of black tongs. She selects several sandwiches and places them daintily on the plate before adding some cold cuts and a handful of salad.

She then thrusts the plate toward me. I grab it, startled.

"Eat this."

It's my grandmother. Tall and intimidating, and I'm not easily intimidated.

I hate direct orders, always have. Yet I pick up a fork and stab it into some lettuce. She watches me take a few large bites of everything before nodding in what appears to be satisfaction.

Then she goes back to mingling without saying another word to me.

It's the first time we've spoken since I was really young.

What a strange day. I feel flashes of déjà vu but know that there is absolutely no way that I've been here before. It's so uncomfortable. Gran seems so ethereal and unapproachable in the flesh. She's nothing like Dad's mother. Granny Knox bakes banana bread and gives me watered-down fruit punch. She always sneaks some money into my pocket before I leave. She lives alone in a bungalow outside London and calls to chat on the phone. She'll talk about her neighbors and friends from church, as well as whatever has been going on at the Women's Institute.

My other grandmother is not like that at all. I can see that much.

Then there's Aunt Opal. Comes late, leaves early, and says not one word to a single person.

And then him. The Stranger.

I glance down at the business card one last time. It's been a strange day, all in all.

What's one more strange thing before night falls?

CHAPTER FOUR

AVIZANDUM

I slip away without anyone noticing.

Half an hour later, I'm in the middle of town and the sun has almost set. I'm standing by the National Museum of Scotland, on the southern end of George IV Bridge. An old building from long ago with a new modern addition stuck on next to it. That's not uncommon in this town. While things are flattened back in London to make way for new luxury apartments, Edinburgh likes to keep its buildings low to the ground. Nothing is wasted or seemingly forgotten.

There are coffee shops and cafés dotted about, places that Dad says will transform into performance venues when the festival arrives in August. As darkness creeps over, I send a quick text to Mum.

I have to send one every hour, letting her know that I'm all right.

This is the third one I've sent, and none have been read.

I can see a fight happening outside a place called Frankenstein Pub, down the road. The doorman is trying to separate two furious visitors, while they desperately attempt to land punches on each other. I grimace, but I'm too fascinated to stop watching.

Two tall blond people exit the pub, dodging the fight but watching it with glee and appreciation. I squint at them. They're a strange pair. Their enjoyment is even stranger. They watch the two men swing at each other before they turn to leave. Once they are out of sight, the argument starts to wind down. I cannot hear what is being said, but I watch the two men go separate ways.

A car rattles by so quickly, I let out a noise of surprise and leap back. As I do, my eyes lock onto a small mounted statue directly across from me, on the other side of the road. It's Greyfriars Bobby. The most famous dog in Scotland. A true-to-life bronze statue of the Skye Terrier on a granite water fountain. Since moving to Edinburgh, I've learned he's extremely famous here. He was a little dog in the 1800s who sat by his dead master's grave for years. The city adopted him, and now there's a statue honoring him. I watch the little bronze creature with mild interest.

Then, in one tired blink, everything changes.

My memory is sometimes a slow cooker, full of different ingredients. Some flavors and scents are too powerful to ever be lost. I remember things that matter. Things that have impact. The good and the bad.

And this is one moment that I know will become a fork in the road. A moment with a "before" and an "after."

The bronze statue of the dog shakes its little shoulders, peers down at the ground, and takes a moment before twitching its golden nose. Then it leaps, daintily, onto the street below. Greyfriars Bobby has come to life!

I can feel that my body is taut, and every bit as still as the statue ought to be. As it was only a moment ago. I stagger across the road, luckily avoiding the traffic, and approach the impossible scene.

The dog shakes himself, as if his bronze fur is somehow wet. Then he begins to trot down Candlemaker Row, toward a small shop front that is painted entirely red. A sandy, dusky sort of red.

I gaze around. No one else is watching. I'm desperate to spot someone else staring at this moving bronze creature, wanting to see them react with the same shock and disbelief that I'm feeling. But there is no one, and I cannot dwell on it because I don't want to lose sight of the dog. My legs are slightly stumbly and my coordination is worse than usual as I stagger down the sloping lane toward the shop front.

The enchanted statue settles itself happily right by the front door of Avizandum, the bookshop. As if it is somehow guarding the entrance. I glance back to the granite fountain where the statue usually sits. People walk by it as if nothing has changed. No one notices a thing. No one points or even gives it a second glance.

I approach the strange creature and lean down, my hand outstretched to touch it. It reacts like a live dog, tilting its head. Its ears prick up as I rest my hand on its back. I almost expect to touch fur, but it's still hard bronze. As if I were touching the statue, as usual.

But it's alive. That's undisputed.

Though I cannot explain how.

I'm about to step inside the shop when I realize something. I have no memory of what the Stranger looked like. Nothing. I'm usually all right with faces (less so with names). But when I try to conjure up an image of the Stranger, nothing comes to me. It feels both unfamiliar and familiar.

Still. I open the door and step inside.

It's dusty. My nose pinches the moment I'm indoors. It's also dark like a cave. Only a few candles lit, not enough light to determine how deep the shop is. I feel a twist of fear within me and I have to remind myself that Aunt Leanna and Marley are only around the corner in the Grassmarket. While we may not speak or be close, they're still family. Surely they won't let anything happen to me.

Besides, I have a bronze guard dog right outside.

A match is struck, illuminating a man in the dark.

The Stranger. I suddenly recognize him. Now that he's in front of me again, I can't understand how I forgot the high cheekbones and the flinty eyes.

"You *are* brave, Ramya," he says admiringly.

"Yeah, well," I say, shrugging. "Put some more lights on and tell me what my grandpa left me."

His lips twitch and then he obliges the first part of my demand. He lights a few more candles and nods toward the door. "Like the dog?"

I swallow nervously. "Is it the real Bobby?"

"No," he says, as if that's a ridiculous notion. As if the fact that we're discussing a magical, moving creature of stone is not strange at all. "He's a statue. Enchanted to appear lifelike."

The casual, flippant way he uses the term "enchanted" makes my breath catch. I want so badly to believe that it's true. I rattle through all the ways in which the statue could be a trick, but I come up short. The way its solid shoulders moved, its quickness and its agility; this is no trick.

"A medusa hex," he says, as if I am supposed to know what that means. He starts to rummage around behind the front desk of the shop. "Quite extraordinary, really. Not something any old witch could cast."

His eyes don't flicker up to catch my reaction, but I quell it anyway. I want to keep my astonishment and my curiosity hidden.

"A medusa hex?" I repeat, my voice giving me away as it cracks upon saying the words.

"Yes. Animating stone, turning things *into* stone. Or any other material you fancy, really. Either can be called a medusa hex. But as I said, very difficult. Friend of mine did that one outside and I've never seen her equal. She was quite extraordinary."

I cast my eyes around the dimly lit shop. A tad afraid that said witch might jump out from behind a bookshelf or the desk.

"Here we are!" sings the Stranger, laying something large and solid out in front of us. He dramatically blows some dust from it and then unwraps whatever is inside. After he has moved away the parcel paper, a large brown book is revealed. It is plain. Nothing written on the front. It appears to be heavy and the binding is old-fashioned.

"A book," I say lifelessly.

He arches an eyebrow at me. "That's quite a tone to use inside a bookshop."

"Sorry," I say defensively. "I was expecting some-thing a bit more . . ."

My voice trails off as I realize that I have no idea what I was expecting.

"Open it," the Stranger says.

I hesitate before obeying. I really don't like direct orders. Especially on funeral days. And days when you're supposed to be completely fine about learning that witchcraft may, in fact, be real.

But curiosity takes over. I open the book.

To find blank pages.

I feel dismay, then disappointment and then an-ger. I glare up at the Stranger.

"There's nothing inside," I snap.

He watches me for a moment. Then he points to the door.

"You saw that dog move, didn't you?"

"Yes," I answer, raising my chin and staring him down. "I watched it come to life and jump down from the fountain. I saw it with my own eyes."

"Did anyone else see it?"

"No," I reply, remembering how unmoved every-one around me was. How no one could seem to see what was going on, except me. "No one else re-acted."

Something warm, but hard to pin down, flashes across his face. The candlelight flickers and the air in the room shifts into something new, something

I have never felt before. When he speaks, it is with a breathless voice that promises something remarkable, and a little frightening.

"Ramya, you have something this city needs. And it's something that's going to change everything."

CHAPTER FIVE

GLAMOUR

I step away from the desk. Away from the empty book. I back up against the door, needing to feel it behind me. Needing to know that I can grab the handle and run at any moment. The Stranger is watching me steadily, the same way the occupational therapist watched me after telling me that I had dyspraxia.

Learning difficulties and magic are equally mysterious to me. To know that I might have both in me is too much to think about right at this moment.

"Magic isn't real," I breathe.

"That's what Sir Arthur Conan Doyle said when I met him," the Stranger says reflectively. "He could see fae but didn't want to believe it. I did advise him not to mention his gifts to anyone else, but Arthur was never one for being told what to do."

I blink. "Excuse me?"

He places a long finger on the book and pushes it one inch closer to me. "How much do you know about this city, Ramya?"

I can feel myself scowling, annoyed by the subject change. "A bit."

"An old town and a new town, crushed together among the remains of three once-great volcanos. Witch-hunting. Ancient water passing through it all."

And moving statues, I think.

"How often do you look at the people around here, Ramya?"

For some strange reason, the question frightens me. "Enough."

"Really?" he presses, his eyes sparkling. "Ever notice anything interesting?"

I stiffen. "No. I don't like to stare at people."

For a quick second, I expect him to be surprised or confused. Instead, he nods as though I'm confirming something he already knew.

"Can you say why that is, Ramya?"

I hate the questions. The use of my name. My gaze lands on the book once again.

"You don't like to look people in the eye," he says

softly. "Or sometimes, even at all. And you know why."

I feel shaken. My hands are fists. My toes are curled.

"You know why, Ramya," he repeats. "You saw something once that terrified you and now you never want to see again."

My head throbs. I want to press something cold against my forehead, to distract all my nerve endings from the pain. "I don't know what you mean."

"Yes, you do."

I don't want to remember that. Not today. Not any day. But especially not today. Not when he's gone, and before I was ever able to know him.

He opens the book and taps the first page. "Look again. Look harder."

I can hear the flickering of the candles and the gentle rain that has started to fall outside the cozy little bookshop. I step closer, releasing something in me. Letting my internal grip loosen on something I've been too afraid to see all these years.

I touch the first page.

My name appears. In beautiful cursive. It makes me gasp and snatch up the book, holding it tightly to my stomach.

The Stranger smirks. "He wanted to make sure no one but you could read it."

I squeeze it harder. "What's in here?"

"Everything that you need to know."

I watch as the Stranger turns away. He starts putting on a black coat that slides on like a second skin, shining like oil. "You won't tell me."

"Ramya, I'm a bookseller. We don't tell people things; we give them the tools so that they can tell themselves."

I thought he said he was a lawyer? I grimace and glance down at the business card that I'm suddenly clutching in my fist again. "Can I only find you here?"

I almost drop the card as the name of the bookshop vanishes, leaving a plain black card. I bark out a noise of astonishment.

The Stranger is gone.

Lawyer. Bookseller. Stranger. Someone who came to my grandpa's funeral with a wolflike smile and dark glasses and changed everything.

I stumble out of the shop, still gripping the book. I check my phone. Mum has checked the messages and said she'll see me at home. That Lydia, our cleaning lady, will be there now to let me in and watch me until they're finished with work.

I look down at the bronze statue. It stares up at me.

"This is all"—my voice aches as I speak—"very weird."

It blinks its metal eyes. Then begins to trot away. Back up the slope, toward the kirkyard. I follow, dazed. Clinging to the book, still too nervous to read it. I'll sit down. Somewhere quiet. I'll sit down and take it all in.

The kirk is eerie. There's fog clinging possessively to the stonework. The dark seems somehow even darker.

I'm about to turn back when the bronze dog gives an inaudible bark, its body tense and its gaze fixed on something ahead in the shadows.

Something about holding the book, having just been through the most peculiar day, makes me fearless.

"Come out from the shadows!" I shout, standing next to the statue and trying to appear as ferocious as I can. I hold the book above my head threateningly. "Come out!"

Someone hurries forward. Someone who seems as afraid as I feel.

"Don't throw whatever that is at me!"

The tension leaves my body and I hiss out a sigh of relief and irritation. "Marley?"

My cousin is standing in the kirk with his arms raised, as if I'm about to shoot him. There is so much adrenaline pounding through me, I consider lobbing the book at his head anyway.

"What are you doing here?" I snap.

"Nothing! I come here to think. What are *you* doing here?"

My grip tightens on the book and my eyes dart to the statue. Which then makes me pause. I glance back to my cousin. He has not given any indication that he can see Bronze Bobby.

"Marley?"

He is nervous of me. "Yeah?"

I point to Bobby, who is scratching his ear with his leg. A complete impossibility, but that is what the statue is doing. "Do you see that?"

Marley stares at the general area I'm pointing toward. My blood chills when I see how unfocused his gaze is. Either he's a brilliant actor, or he really cannot see the enchanted dog.

"What?" Marley asks. He is baffled and clearly scared. As though getting the answer wrong will provoke me somehow.

"You don't see it?"

"See what? I see grass."

I hug the book to me. "Swear?"

This is the first real conversation we have ever had. We have been characters to each other. Names and faces that the adults in our life throw around, but this is the first time we've been alone.

He looks at me earnestly. "Swear."

At that, I know he's telling the truth. Even without knowing him.

"Come on," I say to both Marley and the dog. I turn and dash out of the kirk, toward the empty fountain.

"Now what do you see?"

Marley regards the granite and says, "A statue."

"Of what?"

"Of a dog. Of Bobby."

I let out a puff of frustration. "No, you don't. It's empty. The dog is there!"

I point to Bobby, who gives me a bemused blink before hopping right back onto his platform. Marley's eyes do not follow the dog as he moves.

"He came to life," I say. "I know it sounds mad—"

"It doesn't."

I shut up, staring at him. "What?"

"It doesn't sound mad," he repeats. Then he nods at the book. "That's from Grandpa."

"Yes."

"So . . . you know?"

"No!" I explode. "I don't know. I don't know why this statue came to life and ran around the place. I don't know why I can see it and you can't! I don't know why Grandpa left me this book. I don't know anything about this weird, strange place and I don't think I want to."

Marley throws a glance down Candlemaker Row. "Mum can explain it better than me."

Aunt Leanna.

"Does everyone know but me?" I murmur, feeling the need to grab onto the fountain. I stare up at Bobby as he freezes back into a motionless statue. No sign of magic now.

"No," Marley says consolingly. "It's . . . complicated."

I take in the street. It's quiet. But people still mill about, going into pubs and restaurants. They are all completely relaxed. No part of their world has been taken away from them. They're oblivious to the fact that I'm currently in a different life. Not at all like the one I woke up with this morning.

"Mum is making really good hash browns right now."

The remark is so surreal, it makes me laugh. "I'm sorry?"

"Come inside. To our place, I mean."

I hesitate. I don't like the loss of control. Needing to rely on other people for information.

But if I have any hope of ever making sense of this afternoon, I don't have much of a choice. "Fine."

We walk, somewhat awkwardly, down the lane toward the Grassmarket. Aunt Leanna's flat is above her shop, and it's right around the bend in the lane, at the corner of the market. I want to say something to Marley. I want him to know how confusing this all is. How his calm demeanor is almost insulting.

But I say nothing. I've never known how to talk to any of my family.

"Here," Marley says, opening the old, splintering door of the shop and leading me inside. He doesn't bother to switch on any light, but the stairs at the back of the shop are lit. I catch quick glimpses of tarot cards, gemstones, and other strange objects that are dotted around the room.

Marley thunders up the stairs, two at a time. I follow more slowly. Stairs are tricky. If I'm not concentrating, I can easily lose my footing.

"Mum!" Marley bellows cheerfully. "Back!"

I make a mental note to ask him why he was hiding in Greyfriars Kirk. I follow him, arriving in the upstairs flat. A large kitchen is a tornado of brilliant smells. Delicious, warm smells that soothe the chill I caught outside.

"Did Gran go home?" Marley asks, sauntering over to Leanna. She has her back to us, her blond hair in a messy bun, and she's wearing a tattered apron.

"Yeah, she left after the reception, sweets," Leanna says, stirring the pot in front of her on the stove. She still doesn't know that I'm here. "And Ren had to check on something at the gallery."

"Oh," Marley says, disappointed. "Well, look who I found!"

"Hmm?" Leanna looks to him, confused. Then she turns. Upon seeing me, standing there in the doorway, she lets out a shriek and drops the plate of onions she was holding.

I jump at the clattering sound of the plate hitting the hardwood floor. I stare at said floor. I don't feel brave anymore. I don't feel like looking up. However, when the silence stretches for a beat too long, I raise my head.

Aunt Leanna and I stare at each other. I scan her face, searching for resentment or bitterness. Maybe a little anger or even hatred. I suddenly remember all the times Mum slammed the phone down on a pleading Aunt Leanna after she told Grandpa never to come back. I remember when I was six and the Christmas and birthday cards stopped arriving. When Mum would leave the room if Aunt Leanna's name was brought up, causing me and Dad to quickly understand that the rift was too much for time to simply patch up.

She finally opens her mouth to speak, and I wonder if any of those memories are about to come pouring out of her.

"Are you hungry? You should eat something."

My breath makes a "pah" sound as I release it. I glance at the stove and inhale the unbelievably good smells that are coming from it. My stomach gurgles in desperation.

"Marley, set the table, please," Leanna says in a cheerful voice. Her expression is still a tad unsure, but Marley jumps to set plates and cutlery down on the small, square kitchen table.

I ease myself toward a chair, very gingerly. I slide my phone out of my pocket and check the time. Mum and Dad will be going on air soon; they won't be back for hours. Lydia knows I like a ramble—she'll only worry if they get home before me.

I have time.

"Just some beef stew," Leanna says, putting a trivet down in the middle of the table. She then rests a large, steaming pot on top of it. Beef, vegetables, herbs, seasoning, and buttered noodles. It's not like the salads Mum has Lydia prepare.

The smell of the hash browns causes me to grip my fork without realizing.

"What brings you by these parts?" Aunt Leanna asks me quietly, pouring Marley some pineapple juice and then offering me some. I accept.

"Just making my way home after the service."

Aunt Leanna almost drops the bottle, staring at me in astonishment. "You were there?"

I feel relief and embarrassment. Relief that she wasn't ignoring me during the funeral; she didn't see me. Embarrassment for reasons I can't fully articulate. As though I'm not part of the inner circle. Not one of the chosen family members.

"I was there," I say softly.

"I didn't see you," Leanna breathes, looking to Marley. He shrugs and shakes his head, eyes wide and mouth full of chunks of stew.

I'm used to feeling unseen. When we lived in London, Mum and Dad made sure I went to school each day but also that I came straight home. I was not to see a single soul outside our small, local bubble. They're far more relaxed now that we live in Edinburgh. But I know what it's like to be invisible. They even talk to each other as though I'm not there.

Once you've felt invisible for long enough, you start to behave in ways that will insist that people notice you.

"Your . . ." Leanna pauses, clearing her throat. "Your mum wasn't there, was she?"

"No," I reply. "She and Dad have to work."

Leanna's jaw tightens for a moment while she heaps some mushrooms onto her plate. "Oh."

I feel a sudden urge to defend my parents. To explain their incredibly demanding schedules, one that requires them to have three mobile phones each.

But I don't think Aunt Leanna wants to hear it.

"Grandpa left me something."

I'm not sure if she wants to hear that, either, but I've blurted it out now.

"Really?" she says, warmly and gently. "What did he leave you?"

I lean down and slide the large book out from under the chair. I set it gingerly next to the pot of stew.

We all stare at it for a moment.

"I'm scared to read it," I tell Leanna, only realizing that it's true after speaking it aloud.

Leanna smiles in a reassuring way. Compassionate. "But you're the only one who can."

So she knows something about it all.

"Explain it to me."

She must recognize how serious I am. My flippancy has gone, leaving a weird and irritable sincerity. She must hear in my voice how unsettled I am by everything that has happened today.

"I saw the statue of Greyfriars Bobby come to life and walk into a bookshop," I add defiantly. "I can take it."

She glances at Marley, looking concerned, but he's leaning forward on his elbows. He's keen and eager to hear every word.

"All right," Leanna says quietly. "I'll tell you. But there are things that I still don't know. That Dad didn't even know. Things we couldn't see."

"He tried to talk to me about it once," I say. I've never spoken of that night. Never dared to. But I know this is all connected, it doesn't take a lot to see that. That knowing, needling place inside me that I've been afraid to peer into became a wide-open wound tonight. I know finding out what's going on will heal it.

I look around the room. Cozy stove, a fridge with tons of papers concerning Marley pinned on it with magnets. His schedule for school, drawings he's done. Some clearly from younger years, others more recent creations. Photographs.

It's a lived-in kitchen. The rest of the flat is probably the same.

I wonder if Grandpa and Gran laughed with them around this small kitchen table, over stew.

Aunt Leanna and Marley are close. They were close with Grandpa. They are close with my grandmother. All of them share a past, share a host of memories that I will never have. Sometimes the past feels like a room you've walked into suddenly, a space you have not been invited into. Everyone stops talking upon your arrival. Whatever conversation they were having before you entered is private and none of your business.

I've never had a room of my own. Not like that.

"He said I was special," I say finally. "I want to know what he meant."

Aunt Leanna cracks her fingers and takes a mouthful of stew for courage. Then, "You saw that statue move because you have a rare sense. You can see through Glamour."

Silence falls over the kitchen and I stare at the two of them.

"Glamour?" I say at last. "What do you mean by

that? As in, I can see through people who are glamourous?"

"It's ancient," Marley pipes up, wriggling in his chair. As if he's been restraining every inch of himself, desperate to tell me everything. "It's a shield. A magical shield. One that supernatural beings use to disguise themselves. They glamour themselves. So that humans can't see that they're different."

I hate how I feel. Completely agog and miles behind the two of them. While at the same time nervous that this is some elaborate joke they're playing on me.

"You can see through their Glamour, Ramya. That's why you could see the statue move . . ." Marley's face falls as he adds, ". . . when I couldn't."

"Magic," I say quietly, staring at the book. I don't want to be slow. I don't want to take forever to catch on, but this is a lot to process.

I open the book sharply, before I can change my mind.

"We can't read it," Leana says softly. "Only you."

Marley puffs out a small sound of frustration. "I've tried. I've read every book in the library about this stuff. The school library, and the one across the street. I've memorized everything I've read about magic, but I can't read Grandpa's book."

I swallow. Then I touch the first page.

Black ink drips and spills onto the page, forming

written words like drops of water joining together on a windowpane. It's both astonishing and exhilarating. One bronze statue coming to life could be a delusion, but words appearing from nowhere before my eyes is proof. There really is enchantment in this city. It's real.

"Witches," I read aloud, tracing the swooping letters that now make up the word on the first page. My chest is tight. "The Stranger who gave me the book said a powerful witch cast a spell on the statue."

The unspoken question about how witches can be real sits between the three of us.

"Witchcraft isn't like other magical properties," Leanna says in a considered tone. "It's . . . a lot like singing. Some people are born able to hit a high C. Others have the talent but have to really work to get there. And many, no matter how they try, will never get there. No amount of rehearsal or repetition will get them there."

Marley sniffs and glances away for a moment.

I let that sink in. Talent. Magic is a talent. Something that relies on natural ability that can be honed but not taught. Something that cannot be paid for or passed down from the rich to their children. It cannot be bartered for or auctioned off.

"I've done a lot of reading on the subject," Marley says weakly. "Lots. Witches usually have an affinity for one particular thing. Like, maybe one is really good at telekinesis. Another might be good at healing."

"And some are good with plants."

I look to Leanna as she speaks, and almost fall out of my chair as she moves her fingers, causing a wilting flower in a small pot to bloom and straighten, gaining color and life with unnatural speed.

I feel like I've swallowed sand. *"You . . ."*

Leanna smiles sheepishly and shrugs. "That's about as much as I can do. My talents are . . . small."

"Only a truly powerful witch could access all the gifts," Marley goes on, and I can tell that his mother's talents are no secret to him. "And they don't use wands or incantations. It's all . . . kind of natural."

"So what am I to do with this thing?" I say shakily, gesturing to the book. "It says 'Witches.' The rest of the page is blank."

"Grandpa wanted it all written down," Marley says forlornly. "He wanted the truth all written down. He wanted the Hidden Folk to be seen and protected."

"Turn the pages, Ramya," Leanna says gently.

I do. To find that each one has a different word at the top.

"Trolls," I read blankly. "Vampires. Sprites. The Fae. Water Creatures. Shape-shifters."

I pull my hand away quickly, as if it's been burned.

"Is this a trick?" I ask. "Are you making fun of me?"

"No. This was his work. His life. It's why Cass—why your mum and grandfather stopped speaking," Leanna says quietly.

I flinch. "What?"

"That night." She speaks so carefully, even reaching across the table to squeeze my wrist. Lightly. "You saw something, didn't you? That Christmas?"

The memories elbow their way into my head. Slamming doors. Dad's calm voice and Mum's shaking hands. Grandpa's sorrow. I remember exactly how it felt, standing in the middle of the black, wet road. Illuminated by some weak streetlamps, watching him drive away forever.

Then *her.*

"Yes," I murmur, my nails digging into the parchment of the old book. "I saw something."

Marley's head whips between Leanna and me. This piece of information has obviously thrilled him.

"And you knew something was different? Whatever it was you saw?"

I glance back down at the unfinished book. "Yes."

"He wanted you to record it all," Leanna finally says, after another long silence between the three of us. "Whenever you see something inexplicable, he wants you to write it down."

I shake my head fiercely. "I don't see anything. Not anymore. That was the last time."

"Because you don't want to try," Leanna insists. "But you have to. It's who you are, Ramya."

I want to knock all the food to the floor. They don't know who I am. They don't know me any better than they know the neighbors next door or a stranger on the street.

And I don't know them.

"I can't finish this book," I say stiffly. "Marley, you do it. You said you've read every book in the library, so you do it."

"That's just it," Marley says softly. "We don't know if those books are correct. We don't know who wrote them, so we don't know how to tell what's truth and what's legend."

"The information on witchery is very skewed," Leanna adds. "I mean, the history of this city speaks to that. So we can't know how to trust everything else."

"Why do we need the truth?" I grumble, stabbing a hash brown with my fork. "Why does it matter?"

Leanna opens her mouth and then closes it quickly. She jerks to attention, serving more food onto our plates. "It doesn't, really. It was only one of Dad's obsessions. But it's not important."

She's lying. I can't say why, but I know she's not being honest.

"My dad wanted more than anything to have your

gift," she finally reveals, smiling wanly. "He really did. He always hoped you would carry on this work for him. But, Ramya, listen. Magical statues, those words in the pages there . . . it's not something you should go hunting for. If you ever happen to see something unusual, make a quick note of it. That's all."

I stare her down. She smiles back at me, a kind smile. A nervous smile. A hopeful, tired smile.

"Grandpa just wanted me to take notes here and there?" I put to her coolly. I know it's so much more than that. Something important. Grandpa worked his whole life for this information, despite having no ability to see any of the magic. There is so much more to this story than just gathering a few notes here and there, and my voice challenges Aunt Leanna to tell me what the real reason is. Why it matters.

She starts to busy herself with the dinner. Scraping everything that's left onto our plates and then clearing up a few dishes. "Yes."

I'm about to bite back with something, but I stop. I don't want to overstep. I don't want the only people who seem to know anything about all this to leave me behind.

"Your parents know you're here, right?" Aunt Leanna asks suddenly, seeming anxious.

"Oh." I pat the mobile phone in my pocket, knowing that they have the six and ten o'clock news to do before they're home. "Of course."

It's only a small lie. Certainly nothing like keeping the secret of an entire underground world.

"Oh, really?" She is delighted and surprised. "That's . . . that's really good."

Marley starts talking about his day. About the funeral. I tune out my hearing and turn one more page in the book.

Then I stop.

Some words start to form on the bottom corner of the page. The writing shaken and hurried. Someone wrote this in a rush.

I glance at my aunt and cousin, who are beaming at me while they clear some of the table and joke with each other. I smile back weakly. Trying to grasp at the warmth in the room, the warmth that momentarily disappeared upon reading those frantically written words.

I help finish off the hash browns with Marley and let Aunt Leanna tell me all about Grandpa. I slam the book closed. I don't open it for the rest of the night. I don't remember the Stranger's face, it's gone from my memory once more, but I don't try to call it back.

Yet as Aunt Leanna drives me home to Clarence Street, I feel the words staring up at me.

Beware the sirens.

CHAPTER SIX

VAMPIRE IN THE LIBRARY

There's a water leak in our house. It's small. It doesn't always drip. When it does, it's gentle but hard to ignore.

Dad keeps meaning to deal with it, but he forgets.

After getting home, Lydia and I eat snacks in front of the television, and when I finally hear Mum and Dad pulling into the drive, I dash upstairs and shut myself in my room.

Now I can hear Lydia saying good night while my parents move into the living room. Their voices sound merry and oblivious to me.

Unmoved. Merely another day to them.

I look down at the beautiful doll's house Dad bought for me many years ago. Three stories with a detachable roof and real electric lights inside. It's furnished beautifully, but there is only one doll. A little girl. I move her from the bed and sit her in the small living room. There are no other dolls there with her.

I can hear the stairs creaking, so I snap off my bedside lamp and leap into bed, wrapping the duvet around me like a cocoon and facing away from the door.

The door opens and I can tell it's Mum by the hesitation before she speaks.

"How was today, then?"

"Fine," I say, my voice scratchy and quiet. "It was fine."

"Did you talk to anyone?"

"A few people."

Another pause. "All right. Night, then."

I suddenly want to tell her all about it, but the door is closed and her footsteps are already at the other end of the landing.

"Night."

I roll over and look at the shape of the doll's house in the dark. I reach a hand down and switch the lights on. I close the front façade until I hear a snick.

The lights shine out of the small windowpanes.

It is warm. It is happy.

I fall asleep looking at it.

IT'S MONDAY AND I'VE SPOTTED Marley at school. He's transferring large books from his book bag into his meticulously organized locker. It's right next to the grand old water fountain that has never worked, but it looks impressive, so the school kept it.

"Hey."

He jumps at my greeting, almost dropping a copy of *A Midsummer Night's Dream*. "Oh. It's you."

I don't bother with pleasantries. I never do usually but, as we're family, I feel even less inclined to worry about manners. "What are you doing after school?"

He gulps. "I have Lego Club."

I give him an eye roll, but I don't have time to say anything rude. "Not anymore. You're coming with me to Greyfriars."

He can't hide his flash of excitement and curiosity. "What for?"

I narrow my eyes. "How much of a mummy's boy are you?"

He's affronted and jabs me with the corner of his book. "I'm not!"

"Well, then," I say defiantly. "You can't tell."

Now it's his turn to narrow his eyes. "Fine. I won't. What are we doing?"

I glance around the corridor to make sure no one

is eavesdropping. "Your mum was hiding something last night. Something important."

I expect him to deny it, but he nods sagely. "I think she was worried. She doesn't want us to know."

"Know what?"

"I can't be sure."

I grit my teeth. "Neither can I. But I'm not waiting for someone to come along and tell me. I'm going to find out. So I'm going back to the kirk. I'm going to sit and wait to see what comes by. *If* anything comes by. And you're going to come with me and tell me everything you know."

"It's like we said," he explains quietly. "The books . . . they might be wrong. We don't know if the people who wrote them . . . were . . . um—"

"Like me," I finish for him.

"Well, yeah. Who can tell what information is reliable?"

"Give me an example."

"Vampires," he says, after thinking for a moment. "Garlic. Stake through the heart. No reflection. Who can prove if that's true or not?"

I touch my schoolbag, where Grandpa's book is safely stored. "Vampires" was written on top of one of the pages. I realize this could be dangerous.

"I don't know what I'm searching for," I tell him. "But I'm going to make myself look closely at people. It's not something I like doing but if we're going to find these creatures, I'm going to have to. Now. Question. Are they a danger to us?"

"I can't answer these questions, Ramya," he whispers. "Grandpa never spoke about it with me, and Mum won't say much. But the book is a record. Something to write down real information in. That's all they ever say. They can't see like you."

"Then how do they know about all this? Because Leanna's a witch? Which, by the way, is madness. Does my mum know?"

"No, I don't think so. I definitely wouldn't bring it up, Mum told me not to tell anyone. Besides, my mum and your mum don't talk anymore."

We don't have time to go wading through those rapids. "Kirk. After school. You in?"

He hesitates for a nanosecond and then, "I'm in."

★

WE WENT TO THE KIRK after school. We sat for a couple of hours, as long as we were able to before adults would notice we were staying out a tad too late. We waited quietly. I stared at every bird, every passing stranger, and every stone statue with the concentration of a spy.

Nothing. Not a hint. Even Bobby remained completely stationary.

Now we're sitting in the kirk once more. It's our fourth time here. It's getting dark and we haven't, or *I* haven't, seen so much as an oddly shaped moth.

"This isn't working," I say dejectedly.

"Oh, I disagree," groans Marley, his face buried in his knees. "I love being this bored. This is making me miss homework."

I nudge him sharply. "Don't get sarcastic. We need a new plan."

He exhales, but before I can start formulating a new plot, something vibrates in my bag. It's not my phone; I keep that turned up to its full volume in case Mum or Dad calls. I reach into the pocket and draw out the small black business card the Stranger gave to me.

I turn it over to find that it's no longer blank.

NATIONAL LIBRARY OF SCOTLAND

The words shine up at me. I turn to Marley. "Where's this?"

I haven't known my cousin long, and I don't know him well, but I'm learning that he's a bit of an expert when it comes to this city and the location of books. He lights up at the question and gets to his feet.

"It's down the road. Down the bridge, I mean. On the other end. National Library of Scotland."

"Show me."

I've found that Marley doesn't mind my direct-ness. It makes this partnership easier.

The library isn't far from Greyfriars Kirk at all. We make it in, fortunate that it's Thursday, so they're open later than usual. A few library workers eye us nervously as we make our way into the enormous building, both of us a little out of breath.

"What is that card?" Marley whispers as we head farther into the labyrinth of information and books.

"I don't know," I murmur back, focusing my gaze on every face we see, not sure what I'm even look-ing for. "The Stranger gave it to me. The one at the funeral who gave me the book."

"We should get a table somewhere," Marley says practically, gazing around. "Maybe—"

I don't hear whatever it is he says next. My entire body is hot. Every inch of it telling me to run. While Marley points to an empty table, my entire being is stuck and my eyes are pinned on what, at first glance, appears to be a man with a trolley, shelving books.

But he is not a man. He resembles one. He's of medium build. He has dark hair and dark eyes, and a ruddy face. He shelves the books in a familiar way, suggesting it's routine for him.

There is a purple tinge under his eyes. When he yawns, I see them.

Fangs. One in the middle of the top row of teeth, the other in the middle of the bottom. Not the canines—the incisors. Pointed and sharp, like a venomous snake.

"Marley," I breathe, not daring to blink. I barely move my lips. "Look."

To Marley's credit, he doesn't loudly ask me where, or draw the creature's attention. He follows my stillness, watching him too.

"Marley." I still don't move, speaking in a hushed whisper that would please all librarians. "What did your books say about vampires?"

I feel a ripple of nervousness from him. "Vampires?"

"Yes."

"Well." He swallows and switches his weight from one foot to the other slowly. "They're said to be pale. Beautiful. Tall and slender."

This creature is none of those things. He must seem completely ordinary to Marley. He must be completely ordinary to *most* people.

"Can you see his teeth?" I ask.

Marley squints but gives an almost imperceptible nod. "Yeah. Normal?"

It's a question. He knows I see something else. Or rather, that I see through the "something else." The Glamour.

"He has fangs," I reply. "Big ones."

Of course, I've read about vampires in stories. Biting people's necks and drinking their blood, sleeping in coffins, and being fended off with garlic are staples of those stories. This creature matches no image of vampires that was held in my mind.

Yet he is more frightening. His cool, detached gaze as he slides each book into its place. A smoothness of touch that is a drop too fluid. His eyes are focused in a way that alerts my senses, screaming to me that this is something I've never seen before. His flushed face and purple tinge do not correlate with any gothic fairy tale.

The fangs do.

I begin to step forward.

"What are you doing?" squeaks Marley. "Ramya!"

There are people all around, I remind myself. Cameras, witnesses. If this goes badly, we can run. As I reach the shelf he's refilling, his gaze lands on me. He is calm and disinterested, but I wonder if he can sense my heart barreling around in my chest and my palms sweating.

"Need something?" he asks, in a perfectly pleasant tone. As he speaks, the fangs are on full display and their sharp tips send shock waves of fear through me, a primal kind of nervousness.

As we size each other up, I feel out of my depth. The same feelings I had when I was small and looking up at a beautiful woman who wanted me to play the piano. I don't know what I'm supposed to do. I don't know what my grandfather wanted me to do, and I wish my aunt Leanna had told me. I wish I knew why I can see this creature. Why my cousin cannot.

"What?" he says, when I don't speak. "You all right?"

Be brave, Ramya. "Who are you?"

He is so still. "I'm an assistant librarian. Do you need to find something?"

I realize that I'm clenching my jaw too tightly. I try to breathe. "No. I can see you."

A flicker of understanding settles in his eyes. He has not blinked once. He regards me with motionless consideration, and it makes me afraid.

"I don't know what you mean," he finally utters quietly. "If you're in the library to cause trouble, I would not advise it."

"I'm not here to cause trouble," I say, sounding ridiculously serene for someone who is more sweat than girl. "I can see your fangs."

Now he is afraid. Which surprises me. Our locked-in gaze is broken as he glances around. As if he expects a hidden army to appear from the dark corners of the library.

"I can see through your Glamour," I say gently. "And I wondered if you might . . . tell me about it."

It was a mistake to mention Glamour. The fear in his expression is replaced with disdain. "I don't know what you're talking about. If you want fiction and stories, it's not on this level. And I can't help you."

CHAPTER SEVEN

OPAL

Marley and I were definitely spooked. I can tell as we walk slowly to his house in the Grassmarket, neither one of us speaking or even looking at the other. It was more than we had anticipated. More real, more frightening. Petrifying for him because he couldn't see. More so for me because I could.

"He seemed normal to me," Marley finally says. "I couldn't see fangs. I couldn't see purple."

"Glamour," I say, dazed and not feeling talkative. "He was using Glamour."

I'm still shaken while Aunt Leanna makes us scrambled egg on toast.

"A vampire," she mutters as she scrapes the mess

of yellow from the pan. "Only days after I told you not to."

"I only spoke to him," I say defensively. "He didn't want to talk."

"Of course not," Leanna retorts. "These creatures all have Glamour to protect them from humans. Someone with your gift isn't always going to be a lovely surprise for them, Ramya."

"What was the point?" I snap, glaring up at her. Marley gulps at my tone and Aunt Leanna is shocked. "What was the point in telling me I can do this? Why did he leave me this book? If it's all too dangerous, why am I here?"

I'm angry. I'm tired. And I've had enough of adults keeping things from me.

Leanna watches me warily before putting a plate down in front of me. "Does your mum know you're staying for dinner?"

"Yes," I answer automatically. Mum knows this city; she grew up here. She and Dad seem happy enough going to their breakfast meetings and then spending the afternoons and evenings presenting the news. As long as I am home by the time Lydia expects, as long as the school doesn't drag them in for any reason, they seem to be operating under the belief that I'm just fine and dandy and don't need anything. I know if Mum knew about the Glamour, she would lose it. The way she lost it all those years ago.

She knows I'm spending time with Marley and Aunt Leanna, but I told enough white lies to avoid suspicion.

Yes, Marley and I are in some of the same clubs at school, so I'll go to Aunt Leanna's sometimes for tea. No, we don't talk about Grandpa, why? No, nothing weird. Just food and a bit of television. Yes, I text every hour and I'm always home on time. No, I don't talk to strangers.

I know how to dance around Mum and Dad's oversights. I'm managing it with Aunt Leanna as well.

Of course Mum knows I'm here. Dad's fine with it too. I just have to text and be home on time. No, they don't mind you telling me about Grandpa. They're totally happy for me to come to Ren's gallery opening this Friday, I can't wait. I love art.

Lies. Especially the one about art.

Marley glares at me disapprovingly while I dodge the exact truth, but he doesn't say anything.

Aunt Leanna is texting furiously while we eat. I gulp down some water and then pull out the book. I turn to the page that reads "Vampires."

"For record purposes," I say swiftly, "I'm making a note of what I see, as in without Glamour, and then a note of what Marley sees, which is obviously with Glamour."

"Smart." Marley nods in agreement.

I start to write what I know. What I saw. I try to draw the fangs. I explain the ruddy cheeks, the flushed complexion that was far redder than a regular human. As I finish my primary notes, my pen pauses. I grimace.

My writing. My drawing. The effort it takes to do it really shows in my uneven, cramped letters. My hand is already aching.

The quiet, angry sting flares up inside me.

"It doesn't matter."

I turn to Marley. "What?"

He gestures to the book. "It doesn't matter what it looks like. What you have to say is the most important part."

I regard him coolly. He might not see through Glamour, but he can certainly see other things.

The front door of the flat is suddenly opened with a creak and a crack, causing both Marley and me to startle. Aunt Leanna puts her phone in her pocket and exhales slowly.

I recognize her because of the teal gloves. It's Aunt Opal.

She pulls off her gloves. Slowly. Deliberately. Taking her time on each finger. She has bright red lipstick on, and gold bracelets around each ankle. She drops her gloves onto the table and shrugs off her coat of black velvet.

Then she stares at me.

"Marley." Leanna suddenly speaks with forced cheeriness. "Let's go tidy up downstairs and change the window displays."

Marley glances at me, a question in his face. Checking that I'll be all right. I give a tiny nod. He gets up and follows Leanna out the front door and down the stairs. As their voices and footsteps go from faint to inaudible, Opal moves to the fridge. She opens it and rummages around for ice, which she dumps unceremoniously into a tall glass. She then fills it up with water from the tap, takes a long steady drink, and exhales.

"So." She speaks, at last. "The book found its way to you."

She's much younger than Mum and Leanna. Her nose doesn't look like theirs. Her voice doesn't sound the same as the two of them. She's got an invisible birdcage around her, one that says: Do not put your fingers through these bars or you'll get hurt.

"He left it to me," I say softly.

"He left it to an older, more mature you."

I frown. "Excuse me?"

She swings an empty chair around and straddles it, staring at me straight on. No grown-up smile, no indulgence. Nothing in her face shows that we're family. I'm a stranger to her. This is our first meeting, and she has not let the fact that we share the same blood influence its purpose.

"My father thought he was immortal," she says impersonally. "He left that book to you, thinking you would be an adult upon receiving it."

I can feel the angry sting spreading, growing into a thunder. "And?"

She arches an eyebrow. "Running around Edinburgh, seeking out supernatural forces, is not something any kid should be doing. Worry about how to draw graphs and pie charts, sure. Not this."

I cling to the book, glaring at her. "It's mine. If I want to fill it up, that's my business."

"You think I don't know you're lying to my sisters?" she says smoothly. "Do you honestly think I'm naive enough to believe Cassandra Knox is totally okay with her daughter carrying on Dad's weird little excursions?"

My shock and dismay must show on my face because she nods steadily and says, "Oh, yes. Not sure how you've hoodwinked Leanna, but I know Cassandra doesn't have a notion that you're here. Or at least, why you're really here. She doesn't know about that book. Hence why Dad had ulterior methods of getting it to you. Couldn't use a lawyer, oh no. Mysterious stranger it is."

Once again I can't recall the Stranger's face or his voice, but I remember the dark feelings of unease— and of course the dog who came to life, changing everything forever.

"The whole problem," Opal says carefully, "is that these aren't sweet tiny creatures from fairy tales. They're underground communities. They're the misunderstood beings my father spent his life trying to understand, despite never being able to see them for what they truly are. He thinks they need protection. That they need human understanding. And maybe they do. But not from a child."

She points to the book and shakes her head. "You are so lucky that the vampire gave you a warning. That situation could have gone a whole other way."

"He wasn't dangerous," I snap, and it's a surprise to me. I've only just stopped shaking, but I mean it. He wasn't. Not in the same way the stories have always said. "He was scared."

"Scared is dangerous," Opal replies coldly. "You can't count on luck. This book wasn't meant to find you for years. So lock it away. Hide it under your bed. Under the floorboards. Somewhere that will make you forget about it. And don't go searching for cracks in the walls. Don't go hunting for things that are other. They may start hunting you."

I swallow. "I'm not scared."

"Then you're not paying attention, Ramya."

She wants me to put everything that I've discovered over the last few days into a box. To lock all that new information, and all the questions I still have, into a space I can't access. To go back to the world without ever looking closely at anyone. Without using this lens I've been given.

"Grandpa knew I was special," I say. "He saw it. He didn't tell me to hide it. To pretend it isn't there. To forget about it."

Grandpa's death feels like a broken arrow. The initial news struck me hard, a shot to the ribs. Since then, I've tried snapping the arrow free. Only to leave a small, painful part of it stuck inside. Hurting. Twinging and stinging with each and every breath, never letting me forget.

"He sacrificed everything good in his life for a fantasy," Opal says calmly. "How many lovely Christmases around the fire did you have with him and Gran? Or birthdays, how about birthdays? Did he get the train down every year with a suitcase full of presents and take you for a great day out?"

I'm furious as I feel tears blur my sight for a moment. I don't blink, I won't let them come down.

"Mum told him not to come back," I say hoarsely, my voice a scraping, scratching sound that gives away my position.

"Cass has always been the smart one," she acknowledges. "He wasted his life trying to protect creatures that don't need protection, while his own family fell apart. It's not a legacy to be proud of or to carry on. Live your life. Have a childhood. Make friends. Don't go squinting at shadows."

She is a strange person for me to look at. She is much younger than her voice. Her face and body are soft but every part of her being is hardened. Her eyes are guarded. They've found many people lacking and turned away from them forever as a result. I notice her hands. Her nails. They're like mine. Bitten raw, right down to the quick.

"You can't tell me that magic is real and then take it away," I say cautiously.

I want to yell. It hurts. Whatever this is. To know that they all have their secrets and their memories and their touchstones, and I'm outside peering in. Aunt Leanna's shop and her flat above are so cozy. Sometimes I see the two of them through the window, while I stand outside in the Grassmarket. It makes me feel like a ghost. Something Edinburgh is supposedly famous for. A ghost haunting my own family.

Then I'm given this information. A gift. An explanation. It felt like a touch. Contact from these mysterious people, these faces from photographs who are now real and in front of me. It felt like a touch that said, "You can be one of us."

It's all I have ever wanted. My entire life. Just to be included.

There's a price to being unlike other people. People can sense it. I grew up with faces frowning down at me in confusion and frustration. I became a measuring stick for people's characters. For their patience, their compassion, their empathy.

You get tired of it after a while. I know this anger and this tiredness are what is behind my sarcasm. My avoidance. My lack of enthusiasm for workshops at school, or even school in general. My prickliness. A flower grows thorns once it's been snapped out of the soil too many times.

Or when it doesn't get any sun.

"Keep that book out of sight and out of mind," Opal says, getting up and reaching for her coat and gloves. "Or I'll have to report back to Cass."

I'm tempted to snarl a response to that, but I suppress it. As Opal pulls the dark velvet hood of her coat up over her mass of hair, I remember something. I glance down at the book, the one I've just been told not to think about.

"Opal?"

It feels strange to use her name. It's an unusual name anyway, and the only history I have with it is hearing Mum and Dad mutter it in exasperation.

"There's a scribbled note saying something weird inside the book."

"Oh, yes?" she asks glibly, pulling her gloves on.

"Yeah."

"What does it say?"

"Beware the sirens."

She freezes. Her whole body going from fluid movement to rigid stillness. A medusa hex in reverse.

"What did you say?" I can't see her face and her voice is barely a whisper.

I feel a spark of triumph. "Beware the sirens."

She turns, her face guarded but shaken. Her eyes are fixed on the book. As if she's thinking about snatching it up.

"What does that mean?" I ask, tapping Leanna's wooden table with one finger. A finger with a chewed, barely-there nail. Like hers.

She eventually drags her gaze from the book to my face. Her expression becomes a perfect mask, giving nothing away.

"I have no idea."

We both know it's a lie.

I let her tell it. Then I watch her leave.

If she's going to hide the truth, I'm going to go out and find it.

I don't owe any of them anything. Not a thing, I think in a blaze. They are a village. All linked together, overlapping and reaching across minor walls. Their business is known and a shorthand exists between them all. Community. Family.

I'm an island. Across the water. Watching the tide.

I don't need to listen to their demands.

CHAPTER EIGHT

GREEK TO ME

I scoop my tray up in the lunchroom and nod to the server who is about to give me the good slice of pizza.

"How's tricks, Joyce?"

"Tricks are for kids," Joyce says jovially as she slides the pizza onto my empty plate. "You all right? You're a bit peaky."

I didn't sleep well. Mum and Dad got home late and then loudly argued about the leak in the house, Dad insisting that it was getting worse and Mum vehemently exclaiming that it was fine. They kept up the argument over breakfast as well.

I concentrate as I carry my tray to an empty table. I need to be careful; one stray glance and my brain will lose its focus on balance, and it will all go crashing to the floor. Once I'm safely settled without breakages or tripping over, I pull out the book. I've been obsessively rereading my notes on the vampire.

"Can I join you?"

My head shoots up. Marley is standing with his own tray.

"Can you join me?" I tease. "We're not in a period drama, sit down."

He does, casting a curious glance toward the book.

"What did Opal say?" he asks tentatively. "Last night?"

I take a large chomp out of my pizza, ignoring the cutlery on the tray. "Told me looking for more creatures is too dangerous and not to do it."

"Right." Marley nods and turns to his own lunch. There is a beat of silence before he adds, "But we're still going out to hunt for more, right?"

"Oh, yeah," I say assuredly, taking another generous bite. I swallow. "Well . . . I will be going out."

"Hey." He glares at me. "I'm coming too."

"Are not. I'm going alone."

"Nope. You can see through Glamour, but you need me to tell you what they look like to us normal folk. And I know where everything is."

He has a point. If I end up chasing a banshee somewhere, I need someone who knows if they're leading me down a dark alley or not.

"Fine. But this is my operation. If you get in the way, you're out."

He is a little crestfallen, but before I can add something a bit kinder onto my statement, Mr. Ishmael approaches us.

He is followed by a very serious woman in a gray suit.

"Baroness Guntram, these are two very bright ones in my year group. Marley Stewart-Napier and Ramya Knox."

Marley's entire torso straightens as he smiles up at this austere woman. I roll my eyes. He can be a suck-up if he wants, but I'm not impressed. Not even by the fancy title. She has the same expression as a lot of my parents' work colleagues do when they look at children. The need to tolerate our presence weighing on them and showing through every muscle on their face.

"Are you enjoying your"—Baroness Guntram stares disdainfully down at the half-eaten slices of pizza—"lunch?"

I take a large, insolent bite and speak while chewing. "Yeah."

She smiles at me. A grimace. "Don't speak with your mouth full."

As she says it, Marley pushes his plate away from him with a sharp burst of obedient energy and swallows his food. Even though he wasn't speaking, and she was addressing me. I maintain an icy stare with the baroness and continue to chomp my teeth around the deep-dish crust with as much slow defiance as physically possible. Someone once said you should chew your food thirty-odd times before swallowing, and I have every intention of showing this strange aristocrat who is marching around our school just how much I honor that advice.

The baroness watches me, the detached calmness of her gaze flickering into something a little more bemused. A sudden crash, followed by loud jeering and hollering, causes her eyes to snap to the other side of the dining hall. Some boys were trying to throw and catch pieces of food with their mouths, and one fell out of his chair. They are hooting with laughter and bouncing around him like a group of chimpanzees. The baroness heads over with a steely determination, her shoes squeaking against the shining floor.

Mr. Ishmael exhales deeply.

"What's she storming around the school for?" I ask him bluntly.

"Don't talk about a guest of the school like that," he responds, but I can tell he's saying it out of obligation. To be honest, he looks like he secretly agrees with me. "She's an educational consultant who works for the Department of Education. She's . . . visiting."

"Spying, you mean."

He sighs and pinches the bridge of his nose. "Ramya."

I shrug and catch Marley choking down a laugh. "Sorry, sir."

Mr. Ishmael also spots Marley and arches an eyebrow. "Don't let your cousin influence you with her sass, Marley."

His eyes are surprisingly warm when he says it, though.

★

I'M IN MY WORKSHOP, already bored of the workbook. I peek over at Mrs. Burns, who is speaking to one of the other students.

I turn to the one on my right, a boy called Douglas. "What are you in for?"

He glances up and whispers, "Dyslexia. You?"

"Dyspraxia."

He squints. "I don't even know what that is."

"Motor skills, processing," I say with bored frankness. "They don't like my presentation skills."

"They don't like my spelling."

I spot something sketched in the bottom corner of his book. "What's that?"

"Oh." He covers it up. "It's a . . . it's nothing."

"No, it's good."

"Well." He reveals it once more, brushing it with his thumb. "I like pottery. It's a design for my next project."

It's creative. While not yet colored in, it has intricate shapes and patterns within the design.

"It's really good," I say truthfully.

"Let's not be talking when we could be working," Mrs. Burns interrupts.

I mutter under my breath but go back to my exercises. I grip my pencil with a bored kind of fury. My old school told me I had to "earn" my pen license. Then watched as my handwriting stayed exactly the same.

It doesn't matter how many times they force me to do this, the connection between the pen and my mind is what it is. It won't change. I don't want it to. I don't think presentation is as important as content.

I look back at the vase Douglas was drawing. If he can design and make beautiful pots of clay, who cares if he finds spelling a headache?

I can see through Glamour and detect magic in people, so who cares if my handwriting is messy?

A knock at the door suddenly causes Mrs. Burns to rise from her chair. We all swivel to see who it is and I have to physically suppress a groan as Baroness Guntram enters. She wears a breezy smile, but her eyes take in the room like a cat watching a busy birdbath.

"Ah, Ramya Knox." The baroness says my name with quiet intensity. I get the distinct feeling that this lady never raises her voice. She can carry enough menace without ever needing to shout. She makes people lean in so they can hear her vicious words just that bit more clearly.

I'm taken aback by my own judgmental thoughts. But there is something about her that sets off alarm bells in me and puts my defenses on edge.

"Baroness," I say loftily.

"You're in Special Needs?"

My hands become fists. Special Needs. A phrase that makes me want to snarl. "It's a workshop."

"Indeed. I hope you're working hard."

Working hard not to kick you. "Yes."

"Yes, what?"

I almost growl. "Yes, Baroness."

"You know, Ramya," she says lightly. "Manners should be taken seriously. More seriously than anything else. More than these workshops. More than geometry. More than an academic career itself."

Mrs. Burns frowns at this but says nothing. I merely glare at the baroness, hoping she can hear the very ill-mannered words that I'm currently projecting at her in my mind. She purses her lips, satisfied, and moves away from our table.

While the baroness turns her attention to Mrs. Burns, I notice something curious. The other students around the table seem equally unnerved. They watch the baroness with a nervous distrust, the very same that I felt when I laid eyes on her in the dining hall.

A familiar vibration in my pocket distracts me. The business card. No longer giving either the address for Avizandum or the National Library of Scotland, but a new one entirely.

Another bookshop. On Blenheim Place.

I grin triumphantly. Then slide the card back into my pocket.

While the adults speak over by Mrs. Burns's desk, I turn to the boy on my left, Patrick.

"What are you reading?" I murmur, pointing at the book he has his worksheet wrapped around.

"*The Odyssey*," he says, speaking without moving his lips. "It's a poem."

My face must reveal exactly what I think of poetry because he gives a quiet, shallow laugh.

"Not that kind of poem," he amends.

It has illustrations, I notice. There is one of a ship sailing against crashing waves, with many men on board. The boat is surrounded by women who look like evil mermaids, all trying to climb onto the vessel.

"What are those?" I ask, unable to take my eyes away from the book's drawing.

"This is a good part," he says enthusiastically.

"Odysseus, he's the main character, he's tied to the mast of his ship while his crew all block their ears—"

"Why?" I interrupt.

"So they don't drown themselves."

Mrs. Burns laughs loudly at something the baroness says. I check that we're safe to keep whispering before leaning closer. "Why would they drown themselves?"

Patrick points to the sea creatures. "Because of the sirens."

The air freezes inside my lungs, causing them to ache. "Sirens?"

He points again to the black-and-white illustration. "Those are the sirens. They can make people do things that they don't want to do."

I stare at the creatures pictured. They are beautiful but sinister, with teeth bared and eyes bright. They are purely intent on dragging the sailor into the water and there is something so chilling about the sight, I find myself forgetting to breathe.

Sirens.

I'm out of my seat. I can hear my name being called but I'm already running. To the reading corner by the drama studio; I know that's where he goes during the second half of lunch hour.

I catch him on a beanbag, reading a textbook on Celtic folklore.

"Marley!"

He looks up and casts the book to one side, clearly able to read the urgency in my face. "What have you found?"

I flash the business card. "We need to get here after school. Where is Blenheim Place?"

"Near the Playhouse," he says without much hesitation. "Mum takes me to the theater there sometimes. It's not far from your edge of town."

"We have to leave the second the bell rings."

"Why, what have you got?"

"Sirens." I put away the card once more, staring into Marley's eyes. Eyes that are like Aunt Leanna's and my mum's. "I think I'm looking for sirens."

Marley nods but he seems knocked back by the word. "There's nothing about them in the book, but—"

"Yes, there is."

His words die and he stares at me. "What?"

"They are mentioned. In a corner. Down on the bottom of a page. It just said, 'Beware the sirens.'"

I feel every inch of me pulsing with excitement and readiness. We have to get going. We have to find the next clues. Have to find out what all of this means, what our grandfather wanted us to know.

"Sirens are ancient in mythology," Marley eventually manages to say. "They—"

"Make people do things they don't want to do," I complete for him. "Yes."

The end-of-lunch bell rings. We both start at the sound.

"Meet me at the water fountain that doesn't work," I tell him firmly. "Because we need to go."

CHAPTER NINE

THE HULDER UNDER THE BRIDGE

Marley's directions, and the card, lead us to a two-story bookshop on the corner of Blenheim Place. The October light is dim all around us, but the shop shines with inviting windows and an inner glow. The ground floor is all one room, full of tables and tall shelves of books. I cast a glance around and then head for the wooden stairs at the back. There are words painted on the wall, telling us that there are more books upstairs.

Marley clambers up behind me. The top floor is made up of many rooms, each one with wall-to-wall books.

We enter one that's empty. Or at least, I thought it was.

A ladder slides into view, sweeping across the wall of books.

"Afternoon, Ramya. Afternoon, Marley."

The Stranger is astride the ladder, wearing a grin like we're old friends who have bumped into each other in the Crime section. He is holding a book with the title *Sacrifice: Loving Is Something We Do, Not Something We Feel*. He catches me reading and his face morphs into an expression of faux incredulity.

"It's so good, Ramya. You should read it. Not the biggest fan of the self-help section usually, but I had to pick this one up."

"Got your message," I say bluntly, patting the pocket with the business card and ignoring everything he just said. "What's the deal?"

"You aren't going to introduce me to your cousin?"

"Marley, this is the Stranger," I say, not looking away from the man in black looming over us on a bookshop ladder. "Stranger, this is my cousin, Marley. Now, what am I here for?"

"Should we be talking to a stranger?" Marley asks from behind me while he eyes our odd companion.

"No, not as a rule," I say honestly. "But there are two booksellers ten feet away. If he tries anything, play a scared child."

"Right now, I am a scared child."

"My grandfather wanted you to give me the book

because he didn't trust lawyers or the rest of the family to get it to me," I say, staring up at the Stranger. "Didn't he?"

The Stranger turns a page of his book with insolent laziness. "Does anyone really trust lawyers?"

"He wanted me to have the book now. He knew waiting until I'm older would be too late."

"Very good, Ramya."

"But why? What's the urgency?"

A bookseller enters the room, holding a blue teapot with white polka dots. "Want a brew?"

"I'd love one!" the Stranger announces heartily. "That's what I love about this bookshop. Tea while you browse."

I open my mouth to ask the question again, but he keeps talking, in a very pointed tone.

"Any answer to any question could probably be found inside a bookshop," he says silkily. "Where is the best travel location for getting over a broken heart? How do I make ratatouille? How can I repair a rift in my family?"

His hand moves so quickly. He's suddenly holding a copy of *The Odyssey*.

"And, of course, the one true question. Who am I?"

I stare up at him, knowing that the bookseller has backed out of the room in bemusement and Marley is radiating nervousness beside me. "I know who I am."

He smiles. He's winning this game. Whatever it is. "You wouldn't be here if that were true."

I'm tempted to topple the ladder.

"Marley has read every book in the world," I say tightly. "But who knows what's true and what's fiction? Where can I find the real thing?"

"I'll give you a clue . . . if you promise not to scare them off the way you did that poor vampire."

I bristle. "You heard about that?"

"The magical community is small," he says, shrugging. "Don't earn yourself a bad reputation. It never hurts to be charming."

I laugh at that, a loud and harsh sound that surprises even me. I've cut my teeth on bad reputations. When you've grown up with "What are we going to do with you?" and "Why do you do this to us?" you give up on the idea of pleasing people. It turns into something unreachable and unknowable. It was only after killing that thing inside me, the part that wanted to make people happy, that I felt free. Teachers in London would get frustrated and lose their tempers and something in me would rejoice. Yes, give up on me, too. Just like the others.

When no one has any expectations of you, it's easier to disappear. A bad reputation works like a charm. It keeps everyone from looking too closely.

"Go to the pub under the George VI bridge. At the bottom of Candlemaker Row. Find Erica. She works there. Be quick about it, though. If they spot two children mincing about without an escort, they'll deal with you."

"Erica." I stare up at him, scanning his face for a lie or a game. "What is she?"

"Oh, that's for you to find out." The Stranger laughs, kicking the ladder away from us. "Just be careful where you go trip-trapping, little goats. Would hate for someone to gobble you both up."

⭐

THE GRUFF PUB IS UNDER the bridge and at the bottom of the row, as promised. It's a stone's throw from Aunt Leanna's shop. If we time it right, we can make it to her place for dinner without arousing any suspicion. We've both been checking in via text without incident, but we have to be fast. It's getting dark.

"What do you reckon is in there?" I ask Marley. We're standing side by side in front of the main entrance.

"Don't know," he says. I feel him appraising me. "You okay?"

I stiffen. "Of course I'm okay."

"Sorry," he mumbles defensively. "You seem . . . off."

I don't like feeling observed. Marley is very observant. He reads people in his life the same way he reads the words on a page. He studies and analyzes them, never seeming to reveal whatever it is he has found out by the end of it. He is quiet where I am loud, he is polite where I am brash. He is careful, while I push ahead.

While I might be the one able to see through Glamour, Marley seems to be able to see through people.

"What if it's a werewolf?" Marley ventures. "Must be something nocturnal, if they work in a bar."

My eyebrows lift. "That's smart."

"Thanks, I appreciate how shocked you sound."

I snort. "What else is nocturnal?"

"Let's go and see."

I glance at him. He can tell I'm scared. He is uneasy too. He links his arm through mine and we're joined up, like two parts of a chain.

We walk into the pub. It's dim and quite busy. There are loud groups of people dotted throughout the large, open space. My eyes are drawn instantly to a fireplace over in the corner. The flames are burning brightly, and I can feel their heat and smell the charred wood from where we stand.

Then something else draws my attention. A young woman in a barmaid's apron is kneeling in front of the impressive fireplace, poking bits of wood into place and assessing the ferocity of the flames.

"Marley," I breathe, not taking my eyes from her. "What is it?"

"That barmaid," I whisper. "She has a tail."

He surprises me. I expect him to quiz me or look afraid but instead, Marley's face settles into determination. He believes me outright and strides toward the fireplace with a bravery I didn't know he possessed.

As we move closer, knowing we have to be quick and tactful, I take in more of her appearance. She's beautiful. Tall with flowing brown hair and dark eyes.

But that is a tail. Very similar to that of a cow. It swishes and flicks across the bar floor as she kneels before the fire and as usual, no one is paying the slightest bit of attention.

"Excuse me," I say, trying to appear polite. "Are you Erica?"

She looks up but says nothing at first. The fire spits and crackles, and she observes me with a gaze so shrewd and intense, I'm sure even Marley can feel that it's not human.

"Ramya Knox."

Not a question, but I nod anyway.

She releases a breath and casts a furtive glance around the bar. "All right. Follow me. Quietly."

She heads toward a door by the actual bar. I follow instinctively. I know Marley is inwardly working out where the exits are and how many witnesses are in the building, but I'm too intrigued to be plotting our hypothetical escape.

She leads us into a small office, with a desk that's covered in papers and a safe on the wall.

"Sit," she tells us, pointing to some crates on the floor. "I don't have long."

We sit. "You know my name?" I ask.

"I've heard about you," she says, making sure I hear the suspicion in her voice. "I've heard you can see."

The emphasis she places on that last word sends a pulse of anxiety through me, but I nod. "Yes. I can."

She regards me unflinchingly. "Do you know what I am?"

I'm still not familiar with the social niceties and manners of the magical community, I can barely manage to keep track of nonmagical preferences, so I shake my head. I don't want to offend her by hazarding a guess.

She sighs and gives me one more stare that screams "Against my better judgment," then says, "I'm a Hulder."

Marley gasps. I glance between them. "Sorry. I don't—"

"A sort of troll," Marley says. He then looks fearfully at Erica. "That's what I've read, anyway."

She smiles softly, clearly finding his mixture of

excitement and jumpiness endearing. "Yes. Basically."

"What does"—I'm hesitant to repeat the word, not knowing how to get it right—"that mean?"

"Hulder." Erica repeats the name for me. "It means Hidden Folk. That's what we all are, really. Anything that isn't human, with only the odd exception, is able to glamour. Living undetected and hidden from human scrutiny."

She eyes me darkly. "Until you came along."

I blink. "I'm the first?"

"Probably not," she concedes. "But you're the only one in Edinburgh that's known to us at the moment. And I wouldn't necessarily say that's a good thing."

"I don't want to upset anyone," I say truthfully. "But my grandfather wanted me to know about this whole underground world, and the Hidden Folk in it. He wanted me to make a record. Not that I'm even sure of how to do that, but it's definitely not something I'll be flashing around."

"No one would believe you anyway," Erica says coolly. "A child claiming that she can see trolls and vampires? Hardly anything unusual. Humans will write it off as an overactive imagination."

"Exactly," I say, earning an incredulous look from Marley. "So what's the fear? Nothing I say is going to make life harder for anyone, even if that were what I wanted. So tell me. Tell me what my grandfather wanted me to know."

Her eyes change. Something hard inside them shifts into something gentle. "I liked James. I did. I was sorry to hear about what happened. He didn't have the Sight you have, but he was always respectful. No matter who or what a person was."

"Then *help* me," I say, more emotion tumbling out of me than I had anticipated. More than I cared to show. "Because I'm in the dark. Marley's read every book, but we don't know what to trust. What did my grandfather mean for me to do?"

"I think"—Erica's eyes dart toward the office door, as if she's reassuring herself that it's definitely shut—"that he wanted you to help us."

I breathe steadily. Evenly. Deliberately. "Help you with what?"

Erica gets to her feet and moves to the door. She opens it a crack and peers out at the bar. I can hear rumbling voices, loud laughter, and the clinking of glassware. She shuts it once again, making sure it is fully closed by pressing her palms against its frame.

"It's getting bad out there," she finally whispers, keeping her back to us. Her tail moves slowly, every centimeter of it animated and alert. "Really bad."

Marley and I exchange a look. He is baffled and afraid, and I feel it. "Bad?"

She turns to me. "Yes. Very bad."

"Why?"

She takes a moment to think before moving back to her desk. Her tail sharply wipes off a piece of lint as she sits down.

"For years, something dark has been brewing," she finally says. "Among us. I know you're new to this world, I know your grandfather didn't leave you with much information."

"Any information, really," I mumble.

She nods, her hand reaching to touch a small ornament on her desk. A small horse made of glass. "Did you know the writer of 'The Strange Case of Dr. Jekyll and Mr. Hyde' was born here? In this city?"

Marley nods and I shake my head.

"It makes sense," she goes on. "This city, it's . . . it's not like other places. It's got a duality. A secret life. A dark underbelly that most people cannot see. It's full of creatures that seek out chaos and conflict."

"Grandpa always said magical people were peaceful," Marley interjects, and I'm shocked by his admission. He doesn't like to speak about our grandfather.

"Let her finish," I say softly.

Her eyes shine as she looks between the two of us.

"I don't mean us. I don't mean trolls. Or vampires. Or even the fae. Or any number of other creatures that live and work and die in this city."

I know Marley is confused, but I feel an eerie sort of calm. This whole experience has felt like waking from an active, complex dream. The suddenness of waking up has made piecing it all together feel impossible and disjointed.

But I know the missing piece.

"Sirens."

I say the word, and everything changes. The room shifts. Erica's eyes flash to the door once again and Marley starts to hold his breath.

"Beware the sirens," I say quietly. "That's all I have to go on."

Erica stares at me, her breathing shaky. Her eyes afraid. "Believe me, that's enough. I know your grandfather and his friends think it's a simple matter of making a proper record of us. A magical census. But it's more complicated."

"Starting to realize that," groans Marley.

"What are sirens?" I press on. "Books and stories say they're beautiful women who lure sailors, but that's not the kind of thing I'm thinking of."

They both frown at me and so I tell them.

"I saw one. Long ago. I didn't know what it was at the time, I felt a strange feeling when she spoke. Knew something was different. Then everyone around me acted like fools, all trying to obey her. That's it, isn't it? They can make people do whatever they want."

Erica blinks and tears glisten on the ends of her long eyelashes. "It's not just about what you can see, Ramya," she says in a hoarse voice. "It's about what you cannot hear."

CHAPTER TEN

INCHKEITH

Her words force air into my lungs. "Something I cannot hear?"

Erica nods. "There are no accurate records on any of the Hidden Folk. None that are up-to-date. Hence why your grandfather was determined to create a census. A record that was unbiased and written from life. Authentic."

"But why?" Marley presses.

"Because the stories are wrong," snaps Erica, causing both of us to start. She looks instantly apologetic. "Sorry. But . . . they are. And when the only accounts people know of your kind are some old, tired stories—it's dangerous. The misinformation about so many of us is the reason why we hide. We needed someone to tell the truth. Record the real stories."

"That's what we're doing," I say, looking to Marley for support. He nods, dazed. "We tried to speak with the vampire, but he rebuffed us."

"I don't blame him. You shouldn't either. Humans are far from trustworthy. Especially those who can actually see through Glamour."

"How can we be untrustworthy if most of us can't see you?"

"Some cannot control their Glamour," she retorts harshly. "Some creatures cannot conceal what they are. And for centuries, they've known never to let humans find that out. Your aunt is a witch, yes?"

Aunt Leanna. "Yes."

Erica puffs out a breath and nods knowingly. "Do you know what this town did to people they thought were witches?"

Marley releases a small whimper and I bow my head. "Yes. I do."

"Exactly. Better kept secret, yes?"

"Agreed."

"We are all Hidden Folk, in some way," Erica says. "Even you, Ramya. You are not like other humans, not only because you can see through Glamour."

"All right," I say swiftly, not liking this turn of the conversation. "So what about sirens? Where do they come into this?"

"There is no real network for creatures like me," Erica explains. "We learn of one another in darkened rooms. Underground communities. Whispers. You say you think you've seen a siren? You're one of the few who can say so. Sirens influence their victims with a power that is more dangerous than any kind of magic I've ever seen. They could tell someone to walk in front of a train and they would do it with a smile on their face. I've never met a soul who is immune to them. It makes sirens impossible to criticize. Impossible to document. Impossible to catch."

"Like a kind of brainwashing?"

Erica wipes quickly at her eyes and nods. "Their voice is their best weapon."

"What do they look like?" Marley asks, and I suddenly remember that he is staring at Erica and seeing a normal, human woman. Not someone with a tail.

Erica shrugs wearily. "Not like the books. But sirens are slippery. Their influence lingers, even after they're gone. Their victims will defend them like zealots. Most will never know they have even met one."

"You said it's about what I cannot hear," I say. I have so many questions. I feel we've finally turned a corner in this maze of a new world, and I'm getting closer to the middle of it.

Then we hear a smash, causing all three of us to jump. Erica leaps up out of her seat. She moves to the door and opens it a tiny crack. I duck down under her and peer out into the bar, through the gap.

Two tall and insanely sharp-featured creatures are standing at the entrance to the bar. One male, one female. Their skin is almost translucent, their eyes cool and assessing. I know instantly they're not human. They are terrifying, with long hair and pointed ears.

"Anyone seen a little girl?" one asks, smiling widely with a mouth full of sharp, jagged teeth. "In a beret?"

Someone at the bar mutters something. The tall blond man notices this and raises his cane. He slams it down on the mutterer's fingers, causing him to shriek and howl like a wounded animal.

I gasp at the sight.

Erica shuts the door immediately and moves to the other end of the office. She shoves some crates and boxes out of the way to reveal a wooden trapdoor. She hauls it open and gestures us over.

"Come on," she gasps, eyes darting nervously to the office door. "You've got to go."

"What are they?" I hiss, grabbing a slightly stunned Marley by the wrist and hauling him after me toward the entrance of some kind of cellar. We jump down, finding ourselves in a dark basement full of beer kegs, bottles of wine, and a large ice freezer. Erica jumps down after us and shuts the trapdoor behind her.

"Fae," she says in a terrified voice. "Don't cross them. They're not sweet tiny fae. They're devious."

"I heard they can't lie," Marley says, fear making his voice sound choked.

"They can't," Erica says. "Which means they've mastered the art of manipulation. They can work around that, don't you worry. If you ever see one, run!"

"Obviously," I splutter as she leads us to a hatch on the far side of the cellar. "Why are they hunting for me?"

"I don't know, but we're not waiting to find out," Erica says, kicking the wooden hatch so it opens. Street light floods in. "You've got to go. But come and find me on Sunday. Noon. At the Grassmarket. I'll tell you more."

Marley hoists himself up and out onto the street, turning quickly to grab me by the hands so he can pull me up after him. When we're safely on the surface, I look back down into the darkened cellar. "Are you going to be all right?"

"I'll be fine," the Hulder says, looking up at us. Her face is half in shadow, masking some of her obvious fear. "Grassmarket. Noon. Sunday. Now go!"

Marley is bolting toward Aunt Leanna's. He drags me after him, but I can't keep my eyes from the hatch, only blinking when it closes up.

"Wait," I snap, yanking hard on his arm to slow

him down. We hide behind a corner of the market, eyes on the front entrance of the pub. We're both still breathing heavily as the two fae creatures exit the building, appearing dissatisfied.

"I don't like this," whimpers Marley.

"Quiet," I shush. "Their hearing might be really good."

They murmur something to each other and then begin to head off toward the Cowgate, luckily in the opposite direction from us. We watch them go until they become specks in the distance.

"What did they look like to you?" I demand.

"Creepy," Marley admits. "But still human. You?"

"Pointed ears, sharp teeth. Something off about their eyes."

Marley moans softly. "This is getting scary, Ramya."

"You're free to leave anytime," I remind him harshly. "This is my thing. My responsibility."

"But you heard those creatures," he says. "They were looking for you. So I'm not going anywhere. Not a chance, not while they're tracking you."

"Yeah," I murmur, trying not to seem as afraid as I feel. "But why? I'm only asking questions."

"Why should we trust that stranger?" Marley presses. "The one in the bookshop? He could be sending them after us."

"Grandpa trusted him," I say assuredly. "That's good enough for me."

★

WE ARRIVE FOR DINNER at Aunt Leanna's and I'm terrified that our rule-breaking and secrets will show on our faces. Or at least on Marley's.

However, her partner is there helping with preparations, and Marley is so ecstatic to see him that he becomes the focus of the room.

"Ramya, this is Ren," Marley announces proudly, hugging the cheerful man who is beaming down at him.

"I know, we met at the funeral," I say blandly.

Ren smiles kindly at me and ruffles Marley's hair. "Nice to see you again, Ramya."

I nod, appreciative of his calm energy. "You too."

"I like your beret."

I touch the orange one I've picked out for this evening. "Thanks." I realize that the usual smell of great cooking is not filling the room. "Where's dinner?"

"Change of plans," Leanna says excitedly. "Ren's new exhibit is providing food at the launch party at the gallery, so we're going to head along and eat there."

"I paid enough for the catering," Ren says gingerly. "Someone should eat it. Besides, I want some young people's opinion on the show."

I control my urge to remark that it's art so it will probably be boring, and I follow them all back downstairs to Ren's car.

The gallery is on Queen Street, which is pretty close to my house. I text Mum to let her know where I am and what we're doing. I'm surprised when I get a response from her. It simply says *Art?!?* and then a laughing face.

So she still knows me a little.

The gallery is freezing. Ren tells Marley and me to have a wander around, to enjoy the paintings and help ourselves to food while he and Leanna mingle with other adults.

"Why is the air-conditioning on in Scotland?" I whisper frantically to my cousin as we stand in front of the first painting. "Is that part of the art exhibit?"

"Yeah," snorts Marley. "It's a performance-art-type thing. A room full of shivering people is a commentary on, like, society's inability to feel."

I blurt out a laugh. A serious woman scowls at us and coughs pointedly. We both shut up, but our shoulders are still twitching.

"Well," I say as we take in the first painting. It's a large white canvas with a black square painted in the middle. "This is . . . good?"

Marley is shaking with laughter. "Genius."

"Outstanding."

"I want five."

"A real conversation-starter."

"Excuse me," hisses the unsmiling woman. "Art is not meant to be funny. I suggest you go outside if you find something amusing."

"Art is whatever their reaction is," Ren says, appearing behind us and wearing his universally pleasing expression. "I'm thrilled they're reacting at all. We want our young people to be engaged in the arts, yes?"

The woman bristles and quivers with irritation, but Ren's charm wins her over and she nods. Then moves away.

"You two," Ren reprimands us with barely contained amusement, making us laugh all over again.

"I think the best art is fashion," I say truthfully, touching a hand to my beret.

"Quite right," Ren agrees, smiling broadly. "Though I do have a fondness for this one."

He points Marley and me toward a landscape painting in the corner. It's a small island in a storm.

"Inchkeith!" cries Marley.

"What is it?"

"It's an island in the middle of the River Forth. It's got this big history and it's completely abandoned now," Marley gushes. "Ren's house is right by the water, and you can see the island really close from there."

The Forth is technically a river, but it can almost be mistaken for the sea because of its vastness. It's no babbling brook or gushing stream. It's a long body of water, about a mile wide.

"I keep promising Marley that I'll take him sailing in my boat and we'll go by the island," Ren says. "And I will, Marley, as soon as the weather is better."

"Soon?"

"Soon."

I feel a twinge of pain. Marley's connection with Ren and the sunny aura that engulfs the two of them, plus Aunt Leanna, make a happy group I have no place in.

How strange that the only place where I feel I belong right now is one where I'm embroiled in a mystery surrounding magical creatures.

I look back to the painting of Inchkeith island. I feel a pull toward the mass of colors.

An island. Waves crashing all around it, warning off travelers. Don't come too close, you might get capsized. In fact, don't come close at all.

Yeah. I prefer this kind of art.

CHAPTER ELEVEN

FROM THE DEEP

"I'm surprised your aunt was able to drag you to an art gallery."

I try to lift a wonton out of the steaming clear broth with my chopsticks but it slips right back down into the bowl.

"It was okay."

Mum and Dad exchange a glance, both of them eating pork and using their chopsticks with perfected precision.

"Well, did you like any of the paintings?" Dad asks encouragingly. "We could use a new piece in the downstairs bathroom."

I try once more to capture the wonton between the two skinny utensils. The island conjures itself up in my mind. "No."

"Ramya." Mum points to my soup bowl. "Use your spoon, please."

I grit my teeth and keep at it with the chopsticks. I'm Ramya Knox and I'm not going to be defeated by a slippery piece of takeout.

The wonton slips inelegantly back into the bowl.

"Spoon. Now."

My hand is starting to ache from my attempts to force my motor skills into overcoming the chopsticks. There are just some days when I can't take it. Cannot take the stares, the comments, or the tiny failures that all add up.

I can see through Glamour, I want to scream. You can't. But I can. So it shouldn't matter if I struggle with coordination and other things.

I can do so much more. I want to bellow it.

Instead, I throw the sticks down and pick up the spoon. I wolf down the wontons and the piping-hot broth. It's delicious and I'm furious.

"Nice not to have to cook sometimes," Mum says in an overly cheerful voice. Dad makes a sound of concurrence.

I stare at both of them. Lydia always cooks our meals. She just couldn't today because she had to care for her mum.

"Half-term break is soon," Dad says, forcing conversation into the silent room like a boat pushing through ice.

"I'll be hanging out with Marley," I say quickly, before they can start discussing out-of-school clubs or boring athletic programs. There's only so much humiliation I can take when it comes to forced teamwork and ridiculous things like volleyball and squash.

I liked dodgeball. I found I could channel all my frustration and irritation into hurling the ball. However, after Katie Hobbs was taken to the principal with a missing front tooth, dodgeball was taken off the books.

"How are Marley and Leanna?" Mum asks innocently as she spoons some more rice onto her plate.

"Fine," I respond. "Leanna's partner is really nice. It was his art gallery."

"Well, that's an improvement on the man who wrote that blog on slugs," mutters Dad.

I glare at him, feeling outraged on behalf of this man I've never met. "That's rude."

"Have a sense of humor," Mum says softly, cutting up her duck spring roll.

"Rich coming from you," I say under my breath.

Her cutlery clatters down onto her plate. "What was that?"

"I said"—I stare right at her—"that's rich coming from you."

Stunned silence falls over the table, over all the

takeout boxes. Dad's jaw closes with a snap and he shakes his head. Mum stares stonily at me.

"Have you had an aneurysm?"

"Maybe," I tell her. "Not that you would notice."

Mum turns to Dad, her astonishment almost comical. "Are you hearing this, Mike?"

"Yes," Dad says, feigning anger. "Ramya, if this is the kind of language you're picking up around your aunt and cousin, I doubt you'll find yourself spending October break with them."

"You sure you want to commit to paying Lydia overtime?"

"That's it," Mum says, throwing down her napkin. "Get up. You're going to your room."

"Fine," I snap, pushing myself away from the table. I didn't know I was in the mood to pick a fight until it started happening. Maybe the sore hands and the inability to win a battle with the utensils have made me irritable. Either way, I never feel like I can back down from a fight. Only swim down. Deeper into the anger.

"You're angry we're working so much, is that it?" Mum asks sharply as she marches me out of the kitchen and upstairs.

No. I'm angry because our entire family seems to know a lot about how there is actually magic living alongside us. Aunt Leanna even happens to have some. I've seen her make plants grow, heal a few cuts and bruises, and perform other tricks of magic. You probably know a bit about it but you're hiding it.

We've reached the bottom of the stairs when a knock sounds loudly and confidently on the door. We freeze, Mum's hand still grasping my elbow. We stare at the door. It's only when the visitor knocks once more that Mum lets go of me and edges toward it, peering through the spyhole.

Her body relaxes a little when she sees who it is. She opens the door.

Aunt Leanna is standing on the doorstep, smiling widely. "Hello."

Mum's voice is stiff and uneasy. "Hello."

My eyes flit between the two of them. Decades of history I have no access to. The cold civility of adults when they clearly want to scream like children but won't.

"Ren and I would like to invite you all to dinner," Leanna finally says, bouncing from one foot to another on the doorstep. I can see Marley in the car. I throw him a glance that says, "What on earth is all this?" He throws one back that says, "If only I knew?"

"Oh, yes?" Mum says softly. I look down at her hand on my arm. It's warm. Really warm. Almost unnaturally warm. There's no sweat or clamminess, only heat. "At the shop?"

"No, on the waterfront. Ren's place. I thought Ramya would like to see it; it's right by the river."

Though Aunt Leanna and I haven't known each other long, she knows I love water, just as I know she loves plants.

"You and Dad are off tomorrow," I remind Mum, tugging at her grip on my arm.

She rounds on me with *that* look. The one that says I'm lucky someone from outside our house is watching. Parents always have to be nicer when you have a friend over, or another adult. They feel more self-conscious about snapping or chasing you with a slipper.

Leanna perseveres. "I can text you the address. Six o'clock?"

Something I don't fully understand crosses Mum's face. "All right."

★

WHEN MUM, DAD, REN, LEANNA, Marley, and I are seated around Ren's dining room table, the strangeness of it all starts to creep in for me.

I know I cannot mention Glamour, or any of the things Marley and I have discovered, in front of Ren or my parents. The navigating of what feel like two worlds is becoming more and more difficult.

Ren's house truly is right on the water. Inchkeith

island looks close enough to swim to from the pier, and Ren showed us his boat in the dock before we picked up dinner at the fishmonger.

Now, sitting at the table, I'm so aware of how close the water is.

I've always had a connection to water. I don't know why, neither of my parents cares for it. I was a good swimmer. A good diver. Yet water full of chlorine is nothing like the real thing. The salt of the sea or the cold of a river. That's real water.

"Leanna says you work in the media," Ren finally says, breaking the uncomfortable silence.

Mum nods and simpers, but Dad seems slightly affronted. I think he's always insulted when people don't instantly recognize him from the television.

"Yes," he says slowly. "We present the evening and late news."

"That's exciting," Ren says enthusiastically, and Dad relaxes visibly at the praise in his voice.

"Yes, we worked at different stations in London," Mum says. "But . . ."

I glance up at her as her words fade away. Mum and Dad never gave me a real reason for the move. They said it was a job offer they simply could not turn down.

"What was wrong with London?" Leanna presses. Her tone is gentle, but the words seem almost accusatory.

Mum shrugs jerkily and cuts up some cod. "The atmosphere in the newsrooms was . . . not ideal."

My eyes narrow. This is new information. I also don't fully understand what she means.

"I've watched the program a few times," Leanna goes on, clearly choosing her words carefully. "I don't know, everything seems a little . . . divided."

"We're living in a divided world," Dad says glibly.

"I remember when the news used to be about facts."

Leanna's words hang over the dinner table like a swaying chandelier that's about to crash and break.

"I think you're picking up on a lot of the twenty-four-hour coverage we see these days," Ren says agreeably. "News feels a lot more constant. Also, social media. That's all."

Everyone around the table relaxes. Leanna becomes serene and Marley beams up at Ren. Mum and Dad continue eating with quiet contentment. Ren's calming influence has stopped a potential conflict.

"Why wasn't Aunt Opal invited tonight?"

They all stare at me. I might be about to undo Ren's work.

"Opal?" Mum says her younger sister's name with a heavy dose of disapproval. "Why would you ask about her?"

"We're all here and she's not," I say defensively. "Just wondering."

"She manages a bar, so she works in the evenings," Leanna says, nodding reassuringly at me. "She would have liked to come otherwise, I'm sure."

Dad laughs under his breath and Mum makes a face.

"I've never seen three siblings so different," Dad says to Ren with a broad grin.

Leanna sips her water and Mum's shoulders straighten a touch. "What does that mean, Mike?"

Dad glances at her, astonished. "Oh, come on. You know what I mean."

"I don't."

"You've said so yourself, Cass. Opal is the black sheep of the family."

I grip the tablecloth and try to resist the urge to rip it free. "Why?"

Dad looks at me. "Why is she the black sheep?"

"Yes."

"Well." Dad turns to Mum for backup but she's staring at her plate. "She's not quite the achiever your mum and aunt are, Rams."

I look to Marley. His brow is furrowed. "She was Grandpa's favorite."

His words sit with us all. Like an additional dinner guest.

"She and your grandfather were very alike," Mum tells Marley. "She and Gran went through tough times when she was a teenager."

"She was expelled from school," Leanna says quietly. "We never found out what happened."

Mum throws Aunt Leanna a glance, as if she is about to say something. Then her face closes off and she looks away again.

"Can Marley and I go to the water?"

The adults all look at me.

"No," Mum, Dad, and Leanna say in chorus.

I'm determined to argue, but Ren speaks.

"It's really quite safe. The guard will still be there. Plus, it's well lit."

"Well . . ." Leanna still seems hesitant. "All right. Take your phones and stay together, though."

"And don't go too far from the house," Mum adds.

"Or in the actual water," Dad says, glaring knowingly at me.

Marley and I dash out of the dining room. We grab our coats from the banister, and I readjust my beret. Today's is bright yellow.

"Come on," Marley says, flinging open the front door.

I'm standing in front of an old full-length mirror on the wall. I gaze into my own eyes. Take in my reflection. I touch a hand to the beret.

"Nice hat," Marley says in his friendly way.

"It's a beret," I say halfheartedly.

I take a step back and glance at the mirror again.

"I look," I say softly, "*fantastic*."

Marley laughs. "If you can bear to pull yourself away, I want to go to the dock and see the boats again."

We shut the front door and run down to the pier. It's not packed with boats, but Ren's stands out. Small, but it has a motor; I bet it flies across the water.

The river is vast and wide, but I still catch myself staring at the island.

"I want to get nearer to the water," I say to Marley, walking along the pier to the rocks.

"Be careful!" he calls after me. Then I hear him tripping behind me.

I reach the rocks. Knowing myself the way I do, I take extra care as I clamber down them. I perch uncomfortably on one and look out at the dark river.

Water soothes me. It makes everything else quiet. I can faintly hear Marley sitting himself down above me on the pier. Other than that, the water seems to sing in this hushed, calming manner.

"Did you know," I say at last, "that Loch Ness has more water in it than all the lakes in England and Wales combined? It's as deep as the sea at one point."

"Wow," Marley says, sounding genuinely impressed. He's usually the one hurling facts at me while I pretend to listen. "Gran lives near there. But she's never seen Nessie."

I return my attention to the island. The stillness of the water produces a stillness in me. I breathe with each movement, exhale with each wave. The moon is out in the dark sky and the water reflects her perfectly.

I don't understand the instinct that comes, but I obey it. I let out a long, low whistle.

"What are you doing?" whispers Marley.

I'm about to say that I'm not doing anything, simply enjoying the water, when we both see something. A dark, shimmering mass in the water. I know Marley sees it too because his gasp gives him away.

It is moving toward us, beneath the water. The moon casts enough light to reveal the dark shape beneath the surface, moving closer at the speed of a great, enormous fish. It flits and darts with an agility that seems at odds with its obvious size. When the dark shadow draws closer, I fight the temptation to run. I watch it approach and I will myself to remain motionless despite my fear. Then I stare as the dark mass rises from the water to reveal three creatures.

At first, they appear to be horses. Three enormous horses. But at a closer glance, I see that they have no hair. Where hair on a horse should be, there is water. Their bodies are made of water, with seaweed for a mane and kelp all around their hooves. There are three of them, the one in front being the largest. He exhales sharply from his nose, emitting a spray of water from his large nostrils. His eyes are silver and sinister.

"Marley," I breathe, never looking away. "Can you—"

"No," he whispers desperately. "What are they?"

For once, I know.

Once, my parents and I were driving home from a party outside the city. As we sped down the motorway, heading for Edinburgh, we reached a massive art sculpture on the side of the road. Two gigantic silver horse heads, rearing. When I asked Mum what they were called, mesmerized by their size, she told me their name.

I asked what it meant. She said they were mystical creatures that live in the murky water. They will try to drown people. Especially anyone who tries to ride them.

"Kelpies," I tell Marley. "They're kelpies."

While the vampire we saw was nothing like the stories, nor the female troll, these creatures are more fearsome and more dangerous than I could have imagined.

"My cousin cannot see you," I say firmly, meeting the largest one's eyes. "Are you glamoured?"

I don't know where I found the voice to ask it, but I did. I'm frozen on the rock, incapable of moving. Everything about them is intimidating. Frightening.

The one at the front shakes his shoulders. The

water seems to dissolve and fall away, and his front half transforms into a human's. An upper torso with a horse's legs, like something from one of Marley's books. Long hair falls about his new shape, but his face is nothing like a human's. The silver eyes remain, with a pointed chin and sharp, daggerlike teeth.

"Better?" he says, and his voice sounds like three voices speaking in symphony. It sends small stabs of fear through me.

"Oh my God!" Marley cries, his voice full of disbelief and amazement. "Oh my God, Ramya."

I take my time. I choose my words carefully. I cannot risk offense with these beings. "How can we help?"

"Help," he snarls. One of the kelpies behind him tramps his foot against the water. They stand on the supple surface of the river like it's ice, their hooves merging perfectly with it.

"Our grandfather," I say slowly, nervously, "he wanted me to learn. To understand all the different kinds of people in this city. I don't mean you any harm. Neither of us does. I can see through Glamour, but my cousin cannot. Whatever you've heard, we're not trying to start trouble."

The other kelpie behind the leader bares his teeth.

"Trouble," says the leader in humanlike form, "is already here."

The sirens. I don't say it. I regard the three of

them. Water creatures that are fearsome in appearance but can shape-shift. They could be the sirens. They might be what Erica was so afraid of.

No. I know it can't be them.

"Sirens," I say, causing Marley to draw in breath behind me. "We've heard about the sirens."

The kelpie at the front stares at me with an intensity I have never felt before. I feel as though I'm being X-rayed. I bow my head, afraid to stare back.

"I'm trying to correct the stories," I murmur. "I'm trying to record the truth."

"And what stories do they tell of us?" the first kelpie spits out.

I feel Marley shift behind me, ready to answer. "That you drown people who try to cross the water."

The kelpie's eyes snap to my cousin, and I flinch at his gaze as it pins both of us into stillness. "The water is full of people who were foolish enough to try to break our backs with a saddle."

I grab Marley's hand. If we have to run, we will run. We're not in the water; we can still make it back to the house. "We're not going to do that to you."

I lower my eyes but feel the full weight of their appraising looks.

"What do you know of the Heartbroken Witch?"

The question from the strange creature throws me. Enough to jolt my eyes back up to his. "Um. Nothing?"

The long, pointed ears of the kelpies twitch. "She hasn't been seen for months."

"I only know one witch," I say. "Leanna."

While sad about Grandpa's death, Leanna seems far from heartbroken. Not that I really know what that looks like, of course.

The main kelpie shakes his head. "Our own have gone missing too."

"Really?" I squeeze Marley's hand and he squeezes back. "How?"

The kelpie moves forward in one sharp but fluid movement, causing Marley and me to fall back.

"We're outnumbered," snaps the kelpie. "By your kind. And what do you do when something is other? You beat and you maim and you destroy. Even the water. It's changing. The skies, the air. You poison everything."

I feel Marley tense, but something in me releases. "You're right."

The kelpie observes me, hostility gleaming from him.

"But I want to help," I say quietly. "I'm not doing this to expose anyone. I don't know what you've heard. What people are saying about me. But I want to write the truth. I want to correct the lies."

I feel something that's hidden crawl out of me. Some secret corner of my reflection I'm usually too afraid to examine.

"I know what it's like to be othered."

The kelpie is motionless. "What are you?"

"I don't know," I reply honestly. "I'm a human who is made a bit differently. I can see you. No matter what form you take. More importantly, I can hear you. I can listen to you."

One kelpie snorts and the other flicks his tail. The one in the front considers me.

"The sirens have had many names and faces," he finally says. "They are no longer of the water."

I almost gasp at this admission. This piece of information. "Yes?"

"Find the witch," he says, and as he does, the other two kelpies dive. Beneath the water and below the surface, becoming shadows once again. "The city needs her. She's your only hope of stopping them."

"Stopping them from what?" Marley whispers.

"Kelpies do not just vanish," the shape-shifter says fiercely. "Someone is hunting us. Something is darkening this city. Your world. Making it crueler, making it harder. They're driving out things that are different."

I feel the cold burn of vindication. "I'm going to stop them."

The kelpie gives a bitter laugh. "You can't. Not alone."

Then he too dissolves into the river and is gone.

CHAPTER TWELVE

THE GRASSMARKET

It's almost noon, and Marley and I are in the middle of the Grassmarket waiting for Erica. It's sunny and we're sharing a pizza from one of the nearby restaurants. This place is called the Grassmarket but there is no grass in sight, really. Nor a market. Just quaint shops, a hotel, a cat café, and a few restaurants.

I glance at Marley's watch. "No sign of her."

"I hope she's all right," he says. Then he shivers. "That creature . . . I'm still having nightmares about them. I thought I was envious of you, but boy. After that, no way. I don't want to see through Glamour. It was creepy."

"I don't know," I say glumly. "They just seemed sort of . . . sad. Under all the anger."

"If you say so," Marley says around a mouthful of pizza. "We should have got Hawaiian."

"If you had any sense," I say slowly, "you would know I'm of the educated belief that pineapple has no right being on a pizza."

"Well, you're a snob. Who is wrong," Marley retorts, looking at his pizza mournfully.

I squint ahead at the west end of the area. It's an old water fountain that's part of a huge stone block, isolated in the middle of the street. There's a small wooden door on the side of the stone monument. Small enough that adults would have to crouch over to go inside.

"What's through that door?" I ask, pointing toward the water fountain.

Marley follows my finger. "What door?"

"The one on the side of the giant water fountain?"

He exhales and puts the pizza box down. "I don't know what you mean."

"I'll show you." I get up and he follows, ditching the box in the nearest bin as we move. As we get closer, I point to the door. "That one. Where does it go?"

"Ramya." Marley says my name with a great deal of tiredness and something else I can't identify. "I don't see a door."

I recoil. "It's glamoured?"

"I guess. If you can see it."

"What do you see?"

"A plain stone wall, Ramya."

He sounds almost . . . irritated.

I graze my knuckles against the door, feeling its solidness. Then I knock. Nothing happens, so I push . . . and inhale sharply as it opens to reveal complete darkness.

"Right," I say to Marley matter-of-factly. "I'm going in. If I'm not back in twenty minutes, come in after me."

"I can't see the door!"

"Well, Erica can. She'll help."

"Ramya, we have no idea what's in there. I don't think this is a good idea."

"I'll phone you. Okay? Just wait here, don't move."

I step inside and close the door behind me, drowning out Marley's objections. I have to use the flashlight on my phone to see in the complete darkness. I grimace as the artificial glow shows I'm at the top of a very steep, narrow, and winding staircase. So steep, in fact, that a fall might break my neck.

"Great," I mutter, gripping the wall as I tentatively start to descend. "Fantastic. A dyspraxic's worst nightmare."

I don't care if it takes my entire lifetime on this

planet, I'm finding out what is at the bottom of these stairs. A hidden door in the Grassmarket is another irresistible layer to this bizarre city.

As I continue down, light and noise start to form. After what feels like an eternity, I finally feel my feet touch a flat surface, no further steps. Another door.

I open it. To a whole feast for the senses.

A space as large and as open as the world directly above. Instead of sunlight, sconces with flames. There are snug booths lining the perimeter of the large hall. The center is full of stalls, brightly colored and all selling strange wares.

Something pink and fragile flits by my face. I jolt to avoid it, then get a closer look. It's a tiny paper dragon, as alive and active as the enchanted statue of Greyfriars Bobby.

It zips up into my face, inspecting me, and then flies away again.

The large hall is abuzz with noise and commotion. No one is taking any notice of me. I step toward the first stall and glance at what's on display.

It appears to be lots of long, brilliantly colored clusters of straw. Pink straw, blue straw, yellow straw, and all of it vibrant, almost neon.

"Welcome to the Grassmarket," the vendor says. "What are we here for today?"

I take them in. A Hulder, like Erica. Staring expectantly at me.

"Um." I feel a tad flustered. "What does this do?" I'm pointing to the pink straw.

"Pink grass," the Hulder says proudly. "Wear it inside your coat, you'll make a great first impression."

I let out a delighted laugh. "So . . . this really is a grass market?"

"Oh, this is the only Grassmarket," the Hulder replies. "The one above isn't for us Hidden Folk. You want the blue? Put it in hot water, use it as a tea, and it will ward off bad dreams."

That might be good for Marley. The kelpies are haunting me still, but they're not my first magical creatures. They were for him. "How much?"

The Hulder looks at me contemplatively. "That hat."

I touch the emerald-green fabric on my head. "It's a beret."

"I like it. I'll barter this for that."

"You don't want money?"

"They don't take money down here."

I spin around at the arrival of someone else's voice in the conversation. A boy who can't be much older than me is standing with his hands in his pockets. He nods toward the stall. "They only do exchanges. Something they want for something you want."

"Well," I say, a bit uselessly. "I like this beret, so I guess I'll go without."

He nods and then jerks his thumb in the direction of the dark booths. "You're meeting Erica today?"

He's tall, forcing me to look up at him. "Maybe."

He laughs. "It's fine, I'm not trying to abduct anyone. She's over in the back. Follow me."

He sets off down the long bustling room. I follow, a little hesitantly. I take in more of the market stalls with their colorful grass. I almost laugh. All this time, hidden under a touristy part of Edinburgh has been a real grass market. Magical straw that can be worn as a charm or brewed into an enchanted tea.

"Marley will love this," I mutter as I follow the boy.

I'm relieved when we reach one of the booths. Erica is sitting there, waiting for me. She smiles when our eyes meet.

"Sorry I'm late," I say dryly. "Took a minute to find the door."

She chuckles. "Doors can have Glamour too."

I sit down across from her, frowning as the boy slides in next to me. "I'm still not used to any of this."

"Well," Erica says somewhat bitterly. "To be magical is to be hidden. Remember that and things usually slip into some kind of sense."

I quickly fire off a text to Marley, letting him know that I didn't fall down a steep flight of stairs and die. He replies that this is exactly what an evil fairy would say.

"This is Freddy Melville," Erica tells me, gesturing to the boy next to me. "He's got great intel on sirens. For your notes."

I eye Freddy. "Oh, yes?"

Strange to see another human down here. One who is my age. Even more strange that he knows about sirens.

He shrugs. "Had a few run-ins."

I turn to Erica. "Are you okay? Last time we saw you, that creepy fae pair was almost breaking down your door."

She smiles tiredly. "I'm fine."

"I saw some kelpies."

The atmosphere at the table changes and the two of them glance at each other, Erica looking fearful.

"They were intense," I add, a little unnecessarily.

"They must have been in a good mood," the Hulder says, her voice a shocked whisper. "Or you wouldn't be here."

"Some of their own are going missing." I try to ignore the horror I felt when facing the strange creatures of the water. Instead, I recall the pain and the sadness that radiated from them. My feelings aren't as important. My reaction seems small in comparison to what they were battling. "They're afraid."

Erica peers out at the market. I follow her gaze. Trolls sell their wares, while the paper dragons soar over their heads. The odd fae move through the crowd, examining stalls. Their pointed ears and quick eyes give them away at once. Other creatures I can't identify commune with one another.

"Who is the Heartbroken Witch?"

Erica frowns at the question. "I thought she was a myth."

"The kelpie said the city needs her."

"Typical." Erica shifts in her seat. "Expecting one woman to come out and save everything. There are plenty of witches in Edinburgh. I don't know which one they mean."

The Stranger mentioned a powerful witch. She enchanted the statue.

"I feel like I'm chasing too many leads," I say grumpily. "Sirens, a witch, missing kelpies. My grandfather wanted me to make a record."

"Freddy." Erica slaps her palms on the wooden table. "Tell us what you know."

"Wait." I dump my satchel onto the table and slide out the book, flipping right to the middle. I write "SIRENS" at the top of the page and poise my pen, ready to write. "Go."

"Well." Freddy takes a moment, seeming pensive. "The first thing that is important to know is that people who have been influenced by sirens often have no idea."

I think of our old London house and that Christmas party. I was the only one who truly knew something sinister was happening, even if I couldn't fully explain it.

"Sirens will leave people believing that whatever they were compelled to do was their idea."

"Are other magical creatures immune to them?"

"Depends," Freddy says, shrugging. "No hard-and-fast rules. Just know humans are extremely susceptible. Very swayable."

"Big words," I mutter. "Why am I immune?"

Freddy regards me coolly. "How do you know you are?"

"One came to my house when I was younger. Tried to get me to do something. Couldn't."

"Thank your lucky stars."

"This witch the kelpie mentioned," I pester. "Could she be immune too?"

"Witches don't see through Glamour as a rule. I've never heard of one being free from a siren's influence."

"Erica." I lean forward. "You said things were getting bad out there. What are they doing?"

She exhales. "Division. Don't you feel it? People are more distrustful. More afraid. More apart from one another. It's not a mistake. It's not a coincidence. Something's causing it."

"So, what? They're secretly influencing everyone to be miserable?"

"No." Freddy speaks calmly. "Secret societies are the stuff of conspiracy theories. Sirens don't work together. But their nature leans toward a common aim. To sirens, other people are like boxers in a ring. They pick one and they enjoy the fight. Once it's over, they don't care about broken bones and bloody noses. They move on to another match they've orchestrated."

Her face appears in my mind, that smile. The cruel eyes. The pleasure she was getting from seeing our pain, our conflict.

It was a game to her.

"Chaos. They want to cause chaos."

"Usually," Freddy acknowledges. "Now it's gone up a gear. There seems to be a deeper plan if creatures like kelpies are going missing . . ."

"Could be a power grab," Erica finishes faintly.

"Excellent," I snap. "So manipulative creatures that seem like normal people are attempting to divide humans and dispose of Hidden Folk AND I might be the only person in this city who is immune to them."

"Your grandpa probably had no idea of the true danger," Erica says gently. "This is all so much bigger than you."

"Wait." I turn to Freddy. "My grandpa knew he was being manipulated by the siren at our Christmas party. He couldn't fully resist, but he managed to snap out of it. If someone knows they're with a siren, could they be harder to fool?"

"Maybe," Freddy says, nodding. "Some people are completely immune."

Like me.

"Others can be very difficult to sway on matters that are quite personal to them."

I frown. "What do you mean?"

"Well," Erica says, rejoining the conversation. "A siren could maybe get someone to perform tasks for them as ordered, but if they asked them to do something that goes against everything they are . . . it might be more difficult."

"Portia knew my parents through work," I say. "What jobs would sirens like?"

I think of the Stranger, his face a blur in my mind. "A lawyer?"

"Maybe." Freddy shrugs.

"A teacher?"

"Too much work, not enough pay," Erica says, shaking her head. "Sirens like being very close to powerful people. Just close enough to influence their decisions."

"Interesting. And that's why everything is getting weirder? What about politicians?"

"Definitely." Freddy and Erica speak in unison.

"I keep seeing people fighting," I say quietly. "In the street, at school. It's not the odd conflict here and there, people are getting meaner."

"Those are the warning signs," Erica says softly. "If humans start turning on each other, historically, a siren is at work. Turning neighbor against neighbor. Cozying up to evil regimes. Or creating them."

I take all this in. "So what should we do?"

Erica looks at me solemnly. "Someone needs to stand up to them. That's all we can do. They thrive on division and all of us being isolated. We need them to know they can't do this to us."

"Hidden Folk won't even talk to me," I murmur, glancing around at the market. "You're the only one. And what about the fae? They don't strike me as friendly."

"They're not. And they enjoy blood sport. Stay away from them at all costs," Erica warns me sharply.

"Duh," I whisper, remembering how eerie and violent they seemed. "But how can I help Hidden Folk if they shun me?"

Erica smiles wanly at me. "Maybe try a different approach?"

I regard Freddy Melville. "Are you like me? Do you see through Glamour too?"

He watches me for a moment and then shakes his head. "I'm not like you."

I sigh and flex my hands. They feel stiff.

As I sit in a secret underground market full of Hidden Folk, I'm starting to feel very alone.

The Hidden Folk need someone to make them safe. Someone to banish this threat.

If it has to be me, it looks like I'll be doing it by myself.

CHAPTER THIRTEEN

PARENTS' EVENING

"Ramya is one of the brightest, and most verbally gifted, children I've taught."

Mr. Ishmael says this to me, Mum, and Dad with proud desperation. It's Parents' Evening. We're all in the main hall of the school, each teacher sitting at their own individual table. We've already been through science and math, both of which were brutal. I think he's trying to throw me a lifeline. One I intend to swim right by.

"Apparently her written work does not reflect that," Mum says guardedly.

"I think that's due to a lack of confidence," Mr. Ishmael says sympathetically. "Her dyspraxia makes using a pen very uncomfortable—we understand

156

that. We're hoping the workshops and the supplementary tools will ease that a bit."

"Yes, I love having a massive rubber tool on every pen to let the other kids know I can't write."

"You *can* write," Dad says, turning in his seat to look at me. "You just need help to do it neatly."

"Don't tell me what I can and can't do," I mutter.

"You see?" Mum turns to Mr. Ishmael. "This is what we wanted to discuss. Recently, her behavior has deteriorated. We didn't raise her to talk like this."

"Transitioning into a new school can be incredibly turbulent," Mr. Ishmael says in his calm, authoritative voice. "As well as moving from London to Edinburgh, Ramya is adjusting to a lot of things."

He smiles at me in that kindly way that makes me wince and want to run away.

"I know what a good student Ramya is."

I wish he wouldn't be nice to me. It's easier to misbehave when you know they expect it of you. That a part of them wants you to, so they can justify giving up on you. He's not giving up, and it makes me want to lash out.

I look across the hall and spot Aunt Leanna and Marley. They're sitting with Miss Bates, the head of history. She's beaming and gesturing wildly, clearly gushing with praise about Marley. Leanna is smiling proudly at my cousin, who is blushing fiercely.

I wrench my eyes away and glare at my shoes. Envy burrowing into me and making me seethe.

Suddenly, someone shrieks. We glance over to see Mr. Cohen. He's holding the handle of a water jug that has shattered. He's covered in cold water, and there are ice cubes splattered on the floor, along with broken glass.

"Accidents happen," Mr. Ishmael says, getting to his feet. He hovers for a moment and then sits back down when other members of staff rush to help. "Gosh, always excitement during these things."

The parents are all asked to attend a talk on child safety while we go through to the lunch hall for a book fair. I move as if I'm sleepwalking and don't acknowledge Marley when he catches up to me.

"How was it?" he asks breathlessly as we shuffle into the adjacent hall.

"Awful," I say flatly. "You?"

I know already.

"It was okay."

I bristle at his false modesty. "Liar. They love you."

"It was fine."

"Oh, sure."

I follow wordlessly while Marley thumbs through books with a fervent excitement I can't understand.

"Look!" he says, showing me one with illustrations. "Trolls. Bet they've got this wrong."

I glance at the picture, devoid of emotion. It's the

same stereotypical depiction as every other rendition of a fairy tale about trolls. Nothing like Erica or any of the Hidden Folk in that market. "Yup."

"Don't you find that exciting?" Marley says intently. "You're like the hero in a story."

"Marley," I snap, finally reaching the end of my tether with his cheerful Parents' Evening glow. "Shut up."

He blinks, taken aback. "Why?"

"In all the books you've spent your life reading, have you ever seen a 'hero' like me?"

He fidgets, rubbing his neck and avoiding my eyes. "You mean . . . um. You mean someone—"

"Yes," I snap, eyes stinging. "Someone dyspraxic."

"I"—he looks sadly at me, clearly desperate to think of something positive to say—"I don't think so."

"Exactly. These stories about the fae and giants and vampires and trolls . . . They may have written them completely wrong. But you're still more likely to find a magical monster in a story than someone like me."

The statement sits between us and Marley stares at the floor.

"I'm not a hero," I say stiffly. "Not a monster. Not anything."

The broken arrow twinges. I lift a book, staring

down at the story of the princess who fell asleep for one hundred years. I remember Dad reading it. The fae gave her the gift of beauty, the gift of song. Then she was cursed. I always wondered what the last gift would be. Dad said it was probably a nice personality.

That's not a gift, though. Cleverness. That would have been a gift. Clever people don't need others to come and rescue them. They can save their own skin.

I drop the book back down with a touch too much force.

The room bustles around us, a hum of activity, but the two of us stand completely still.

"Ramya." Marley speaks softly. "Your brain . . . it's why you can see through Glamour. It's why you're immune to sirens. It's . . . it's incredible. I wish I were like you. I've never met anyone that can do what you do. I swear. It really is incredible. And not just because of the Sight, either."

I push out a breath and wipe a single tear away quickly.

"It is incredible, with or without the Sight," I agree tautly. "I wake up thinking that. Then, each day, person after person tries to change my mind. I feel fine, and then the world comes along and tells me I'm delusional. They make me do stupid exercises; they talk about me like I'm not able to understand them. They measure me up against everyone else. But I'm not like everyone else."

It feels lonely to finally admit it. But it's the truth. I'm not like everyone else.

"I don't believe hats are part of the uniform policy."

Marley and I jump at the sudden intrusion. The baroness is smiling down at us, her gray suit the color of a truly miserable sky.

"It's not a hat; it's a beret," I reply. "And it matches the uniform."

The baroness chuckles, as if I have said something very charming. "Let's take it off."

I know I should do what she says. I shouldn't be difficult. Yet there is something about her tone, about her manner, and about the presumptive way she has inserted herself into our school, and our conversation, that irks me. She was supposed to be an education consultant, but all she does is lurk about and make the teachers nervous. I've no idea how she's elbowed her way into this place, but maybe that's a perk of being an aristocrat.

"I'm not taking it off," I tell her gently. As though she were the child and I were the adult.

Something hollow flickers in her eyes. Disbelief.

"Marley," she finally says, in a sickly-sweet voice. "Hand me Ramya's hat."

Marley hesitates. Then lifts the beret from my head and passes it to her. She takes possession of it with a glint of triumph. I scowl at them both. Her for being a tyrant and Marley for always being too afraid to disobey an adult.

"I'll be confiscating this," the baroness says cheerfully. "I'll return it to you when I feel that you've understood my advice."

We watch her disappear into the book fair crowd and then I thump Marley on the shoulder.

"Sorry," he groans, nudging me gently in apology. "You know I don't like conflict."

"Sometimes it's necessary."

"Not with a teacher."

"She's not a teacher. She's a spy. What's she got over all the staff, anyway? Why are they bowing down to her when she has no business being here? What happened to child safety?"

Marley is opening his mouth, possibly to defend the baroness, when we hear Aunt Leanna calling us. She's waving over at the exit and Mum and Dad are standing stiffly behind her, Dad helping Mum on with her coat.

"Well," Mum says frostily. "That was illuminating."

Dad clears his throat. "Congratulations on another certificate of excellence, Marley. Your mum was telling us."

Marley goes as red as the beret he just took off me. He nods in appreciation and looks down at the floor.

"Apparently the work you're producing in your workshop is leaving a lot to be desired," Mum tells me frankly.

"Good," I say, just as frankly. "If they didn't force all of us into that crummy room during lunch, we might feel like doing better."

"Ramya, this attitude can't go on," Mum says. "I mean it. This school is trying to support you."

"Support me?" I want to scream loudly enough for the whole room to fall silent. "I want them to stop making me feel like an insect under a magnifying glass. Let me use a computer! Stop singling me out in PE! Let me process things in my own time! That's all I need, but oh no. It's workshops and sheets and meetings and constant frowning and making sure I know I'm different at every opportunity."

Leanna makes a small noise of sympathy. "This sounds familiar."

Mum's eyes dart to her sister with intense focus. "Be quiet."

"Well, it does," Leanna replies gently. "Maybe—"

"Time to go," Mum says, gesturing for me to follow her.

I want to ask Aunt Leanna what she was about to say, but I'm being hauled out to the parking lot. I follow my parents and frown as I spot a group of adults arguing loudly and aggressively over by the main hall. Their faces are contorted with rage as they scream at each other, two sets of parents who are seemingly having a fight. A teacher eventually has to step in and separate them.

The baroness is observing with cool fascination.

"Don't look at that," Dad says to me sternly.

Mum watches the scene and shakes her head, muttering something I cannot hear. She flexes her hands and rubs her palms.

As we move through the reception hall of the school, the flames in the small stone fireplace, which has been lit especially for the occasion, crackle and seem to grow more powerful as we pass.

★

THE BUSINESS CARD FLASHED AGAIN, after being blank for some time. Now it was directing me to a bookshop on Nicolson Street, not far from Aunt Leanna's. Marley and I agreed to visit on the first day of half-term.

As we step inside, I'm pleased to find it quite busy. It's not crowded but there are enough book-lovers wandering about so it doesn't feel like we're too conspicuous. I'm keeping my eyes alert for the Stranger.

Yet he isn't the person I recognize browsing over in the corner.

"Look!" I nudge Marley. "Opal."

She is carefully and consideringly turning the pages of a large book, oblivious to us. I head toward her, Marley in my wake. I'm about to surprise her when suddenly she speaks, without even glancing up from her potential purchase.

"Good to see you both in a bookshop."

I exhale, irritated that she somehow knew we were there. "What are you here for?"

"Books, Ramya," she says breezily, still reading. "You?"

"I was expecting to see someone," I reply honestly.

"Not an adult, I hope," she says, finally looking up to eye me with disapproval. "You should be with people your own age."

"People my own age aren't much help in finding sirens."

She slams the book shut and shoves it back onto its shelf. "Oh, really?"

"Yeah," I say defiantly. "I know what they are. I have a rough idea of what they're trying to do. Now I need to prove it."

"Sounds exactly like the kind of behavior I warned you against."

I grimace. "Why were you expelled?"

"Ramya!" hisses Marley, shocked.

Opal does not react, however. She stares me down steadily before finally exhaling.

"There's a nice café downstairs," she says. "I can buy both of you some lunch if it will keep you out of trouble."

It's unexpected. We follow her to the bookshop café. She casually buys us what we want, causing Marley and me to exchange glances of glee. Chocolate cake for me and cheesecake for him. We scramble to a table while she puts soft drinks down for us and a black coffee for herself.

I make sure to wolf down as much of the cake as possible before saying, "My distraction can't be bought with treats."

She snorts, eyeing the tiny sliver of chocolate fudge that's left. "Clearly."

"Why were you expelled, Aunt Opal?"

She breathes in and out slowly, taking a sip of coffee. "Neither one of your parents has told you?"

I look at Marley. He shakes his head.

"No," I say. "My mum never really talks about you."

"Shocker," says Opal, almost too quietly for us to catch. She runs her finger over the rim of her coffee cup, preoccupied.

My bluntness makes me feel guilty. "I don't really like school."

Opal turns to Marley and her face warms. "What about you, Mar?"

He is bashful. "I don't mind it."

"Good boy. You know there's a great *D&D* section in this shop?"

"Why were you expelled?" I repeat the question, cutting in before Marley can get sidetracked by one of his favorite subjects. It smarts a little to hear that Opal knows him this well.

She picks up my fork, stabs off a tiny mouthful of cake, and eats it pointedly. "Self-defense went wrong. Scared the school."

Marley's face is a picture. It's almost comical to see how astonished he is. I, however, look at her with reluctant appreciation for a vague but honest answer. "Fine."

"So," Opal says delicately. "I told you mine. Tell me yours."

I can feel Marley watching me nervously as I say, "Sirens are turning people against each other. As well as making other Hidden Folk disappear."

My use of "Hidden Folk" earns me an eyebrow raise from her, but other than that, Opal's face is unreadable. "Turning people against each other. Sounds very nebulous."

"Well, I don't know what that means," I say bluntly. "But they are."

"It means unclear," she says. "You think a few people arguing is all because of some secret plot?"

"Not people arguing," I snap. "Everything's hardened. Marley's mum agrees."

"Does she?" squeaks Marley.

"Remember, at Newhaven? Ren's house? Aunt Leanna said things are getting more divided."

"Ren said that's because of the news," Marley replies, his tone forceful.

"I know what they do," I say, my voice shaking as I stare down Opal. "I've seen it. One came to our house when I was small. She charmed the whole room, but she couldn't charm me. So she caused chaos. Made Mum and Dad angry, so they turned on Grandpa. Mum told him to leave and never come back. She would never have done that without that poisonous influence—she would *not*. That's what they do."

I slam my hand on the table, surprised at how much emotion is filling up inside me.

"That's why everything seems more divided." Slam. "That's why the Hidden Folk in Edinburgh are disappearing and scared." Slam. "That's why Grandpa left me this book."

I get to my feet, glaring. "And that's why our family broke apart."

Silence.

Opal looks up at me and, for the first time in the short period we have known each other, she seems softer. "That's what this is all about? You're upset about our family?"

My fists clench. "Of course! We're all broken apart. We're damaged. Because of *them*. Because of that creature. Because that's what they do."

"Ramya." She speaks gently. "Humans are perfectly capable of ruining their own relationships. They often do. You can't go hunting for monsters when the answer may simply be people just doing what they do."

A tear is threatening to fall, but I squeeze my eyes tight shut, refusing to allow it. "Mum loved Grandpa. She did. She would never have cut him out if it weren't for that siren. You weren't there, but I was. I saw it all happen."

The tear is still waiting in the corner of my eye, but I continue. "You were never there."

I'm suddenly not able to look at either of them. They can sit there and think I'm crazy if they want.

"You see horses when I see a unicorn," I say stiffly, gathering my things. "I know what's really going on. There are bad forces at play, and I'm going to find out how and why."

I throw my bag onto my shoulder and push my way out of the coffee shop corner, heading for the exit.

"I don't need anyone but myself!"

CHAPTER FOURTEEN

APOLOGIES

I find the vampire in the library once again. I approach him with the gentle caution of someone who has seen a beautiful deer in the woods. One they don't want to frighten away with their clumsy steps or aggressive stance.

"I'm sorry to disturb you."

He watches me with distrust, retreating ever so slightly into one of the darkened alcoves of the library.

"I'm sorry about last time," I go on, taking one step closer. "I truly am."

He retreats a little more, until he is almost in complete darkness. "Why are you doing this?"

It's a fair question. One I have asked myself a lot lately. "My grandpa was James Stewart-Napier. He was human but he spent his life fascinated by Hidden Folk. He wanted to help keep them safe. He tried to keep a census, an accurate record of them, but the only problem was, he couldn't see through Glamour."

I take another tiny step forward. "But I can. I can see through it. So he left the book to me. To finish it."

The vampire eyes the book under my arm and then looks into my face. His ruddy cheeks, tinged eyes, and strange teeth don't make him seem frightening anymore. In the dim light of the large room, he is small. Vulnerable.

"You don't have to talk to me," I say reassuringly. "That's not why I'm here. I came to apologize. I shouldn't have ambushed you. I shouldn't have scared you. I'm really sorry."

Dad always says it's important to make an apology about the other person and really take responsibility for what you have done. If you're going to say sorry for something, then do it properly.

"It was wrong of me," I say quietly. "And I just wanted to say that. As well as let you know, I won't write anything about you in the book. No guessing, no stories. I only want to write facts. I won't make anything up about you. No garlic, no mirrors."

I smile before turning to go. I'm about to step out into the main area of the library when—

"I love garlic."

I spin around. "Sorry?"

The vampire edges forward a step. "I really like garlic. Butter and garlic makes everything taste better. I would hate if those stories were true. I wouldn't have lasted very long on this earth if they were."

I'm so surprised by this admission that I laugh. "You do?"

"Yeah," he says, moving farther into the light. "Not sure at all where that myth came from."

"Someone with no taste for flavor."

"Exactly."

We chuckle awkwardly.

"If you . . ." He glances around quickly and then gestures to an empty table in the corner. "If you have questions . . . I'll answer."

I feel something pull in me, like an emotional thread getting caught on a splintered wooden fence. "Thank you."

As I sit across from my very first vampire, I poise my pen over the blank page and find that my mind is equally vacant. I don't know what to ask.

"What's your name?" I finally say.

He is pleasantly surprised, smiling in a manner that shows his fangs. "My name is Murrey."

"Hello, Murrey," I say, closing the book. "I'm Ramya."

He nods and then splays his hands. "So?"

I feel wriggly, sheepish and uncertain. "Um. Well."

"It's all right," he says, his tone helpful. "Ask whatever you need to."

I observe his unusual fangs. "What's it like being a vampire?"

He thinks for a moment. "No one's ever asked me that question before."

I wait. Letting him assemble an answer.

"It's not too exciting," he finally says. "The sun gives me a really bad rash, which is why I like living in Scotland."

I snort. "Not too much sunshine."

"Correct. You won't find many vampires in Dubai."

I laugh. "What else?"

The humor in his face softens and he seems cautious. "I do drink blood. But it's never from a living human. We also have connections at the blood drives, and they always set aside some for us. Plus, a little goes a long way."

"Mirrors?"

"They work."

"Do you need to be invited before you can enter a house?"

"No, but it's polite."

"A stake through the heart—"

"Would kill just about any creature," he interrupts, grinning at me.

"So you work in the library to stay out of the sun?"

"Well." He peers around the enormous room we're sitting in. "Not really."

"Then why?"

His face is already ruddy and flushed but I get the sense that he's also blushing. "I really love the books. There's no real reason other than that."

"Oh." I smile. I can't help it. "All right."

"Books are like little pockets of time," he says brightly. "Little artifacts from other cultures and other periods of history. You can go to a museum where they put everything behind glass and won't let you touch things. Or you can read a book. I like knowing that some other being pored over the words I'm reading. That we're connected."

I look down at Grandpa's book. I touch it. Press my thumb against its binding.

"Stories are like footprints that can never be washed away," Murrey says reverently. "Even if the print fades or the pages rot or the writer is long gone . . . the story just moves into someone else's head. It finds a new place to live."

I swallow, trying to dislodge something uncomfortable in my throat. "But what if the stories are wrong? Like the ones about you?"

He shrugs. "I don't read the tales about creatures like me. I escape into others. I imagine I'm someone else for three hundred pages or so."

I shake my head, staring up at him. "Don't you ever want to read the truth?"

He regards me wistfully. "Why don't you write that for me?"

I blanch. "Oh. I don't know, I—"

"You can log the truth in your book. The truth about me. Murrey. Just over one hundred years old. Loves garlic and reading. Won't be caught tanning but can recommend you some great travel books."

He smiles but there's something sad behind it. He fidgets and looks away for a moment.

"I'm not a monster," he finally says softly. "I'm not."

"I know, Murrey," I say, just as quietly. "I know that."

He bites his thumb and watches me worriedly. "I know you're searching for them."

I feign innocence. "Sorry?"

"Sirens. I know you're looking for them."

"I'm only gathering information," I say flippantly.

"Ramya." He says my name in a pleading voice. "Be careful. They're not misunderstood. They're not understood at all. If anything, they're under-estimated."

I trace a small pattern someone has carved in the table. "So am I."

"I lost my dad to them."

My gaze shoots up; I'm horrified. "What?"

"Long ago," Murrey adds. Sounding slightly desolate. "Your grandfather . . . he sounds like my father. My dad wanted peace. Open acceptance. One big society with all its different groups living in harmony. No one pretending to be something that they're not."

I'm afraid as I listen. "And then?"

We share a look. "If you know anything about sirens, you'll know they don't tend to thrive on har-mony. Or unity. Or community or family or love or friendship."

I see Portia's smile in the rain. The triumphant glee at a grandfather driving away and never coming back. "Yes."

"They feed on cruelty. On animosity. One of them turned an entire crowd on my dad. They . . ."

He turns away, his face desperate. He squeezes his eyes shut.

"And do you know," he breathes after a long pause. "Do you know the worst thing about it? The cruelty, the destruction . . . Once it's over, and you're standing there with the pieces, wondering how you're ever going to live your life again . . . how you're ever going to get through, move on from the damage . . . they're standing there, laughing. It's a game. The cruelty serves no purpose other than amusement for them."

His words touch that sad, scared place in me. The one that is fueling all of this. "I know."

"Your pain. Your tragedy. It will always be a prize to them. Your empathy, your emotions, they will always be the first thing a siren will belittle. They'll take the goodness inside a person and use it to humiliate them. So that they're too afraid to ever be good again."

"But it's getting worse," I say. "They're trying to make bigger cracks. People can feel it, the world is changing. I can feel it. It's . . . hardening. It's colder."

"They don't work together as a rule," Murrey allows. "They like to move alone. But you're right. Things are bad out there. I wouldn't want to guess how they're doing it."

I'm tempted to keep pushing, to keep digging for more information about the sirens. Yet the sadness that overcame Murrey when talking about his father stops me.

"A siren split up my family," I tell him candidly. "One evening. A few words. That's all it took."

I could cry when Murrey nods sagely. He doesn't tell me I'm overreacting. He doesn't gaslight me.

"I don't believe in being born evil," he says. "I believe having the power to make people do whatever you want, having influence over people, it turns weak minds into evil deeds."

We sit in silence together. Hurt and bad memories lingering like the perfume of someone who has come and gone.

"Thank you for speaking with me, Murrey."

He smiles and I smile back. "Thank you for listening."

★

I'M SITTING WITH AUNT LEANNA, Aunt Opal, and Marley in the flat above the Grassmarket shop. Leanna has made ragout for our second day of half-term. Aunt Opal was supposed to be watching us by herself while Aunt Leanna dropped some orders across town, but she was able to do it in the morning, so now the four of us are having dinner.

Marley and Leanna are enthusiastically retelling their day with Ren in Newhaven. He took Marley out in his boat and, while Aunt Leanna watched nervously from the dock, they rocked about in the waves and had a wonderful time. Neither of them mentions Inchkeith island, so I lose interest in the story and start to daydream.

"Mum." Marley's voice suddenly cuts through

my musings. "Tell Ramya about when you realized you were a witch."

A much more interesting topic of conversation. I look to Aunt Leanna, who smiles self-consciously at the request. Opal's face is unreadable, but she is clearly listening.

"Well, it was lots of gradual moments," Leanna tells me warmly, spooning more food onto Marley's plate. "I would get upset or overwhelmed or sometimes even very happy, and some flowers would sprout. I found when I was about your age that I could mend the odd scrape or bruise. So I eventually plucked up the courage to talk to your grandparents about it."

I lean closer. Imagining the scene as if it were playing out in front of us.

"I was so scared," Leanna says, giving a nervous laugh and pushing hair out of her eyes. She touches Marley on the cheek. "I thought they would call me mad."

She glances apprehensively to Opal, who nods understandingly.

"But they were wonderful. Delighted, in fact. Dad had a whole study full of books all about magic and he thought it was the most exciting thing. I was allowed to give up the violin and focus on magic."

Everyone laughs at that. Then Aunt Leanna's laughter fades and she grows thoughtful.

"But the years went by, and my powers never grew. I practiced. Your grandmother knew how to encourage me. We worked together, but I never grew stronger. I could heal a little. Make things bloom a bit. But I couldn't move objects. I couldn't cast enchantments. I couldn't channel elements, not really. So . . . I sort of stayed the same."

She is suddenly tearful. Opal reaches over and squeezes her wrist, her young face full of empathy.

"But you made beautiful gardens," she whispers kindly.

Leanna lets out a laugh that is mixed with a sob and wipes her eyes swiftly. "Yes. I did, didn't I? Dad always loved them."

"Everyone did," Opal corrects.

Leanna nods and squeezes Opal back, the two of them gripping each other while not saying a word.

"It's funny." Leanna speaks after a long silence. "A little magic is better than none at all. But I did dream about it. About being powerful. Having the skills to really change the world with my gifts. Being able to do . . . well. Well, never mind."

She gets up. She opens the fridge and pours some water. I watch Aunt Opal as she watches her sister.

Leanna turns and takes in the room, assessing it. She waves her hand, smoothly and softly. The flowers in the vase at the table straighten and seem to preen, glad of the attention and animation. Their colors seem more vibrant. Their textures invigo-rated.

"It's a gift to make things want to bloom again," Opal says soothingly.

"Yes, Mum," Marley agrees, tugging Leanna's hand and jolting her out of some trance. "It is."

It feels like we are all frozen. Like people in a snow globe. The dust and the matter around us also still. We exist, completely motionless. The magic in the room like the artificial snow. The only thing roused and moving.

"Can I ask about witchcraft?"

Everyone turns to me as I ask the question.

"Of course," Leanna says shakily, sitting back down at the table. "Ask away, Ramya."

"I've heard rumors about a really powerful witch in the city."

It's not a question, I know, but it causes my aunts to exchange a look.

"Do you know who they mean?"

"No," Leanna says despondently. "It certainly wouldn't be me, if that's what you're wondering."

I say nothing.

"This city is all about secrets," Leanna goes on. "I should never have told you about what Dad wanted to do. Should never have mentioned any of it."

"But people shouldn't have to hide," I insist. "It doesn't have to be this way."

"Nonmagical people hide for all sorts of reasons," Opal says. "I don't always tell people I'm neurodivergent."

My world goes away for a moment. Fades away and then comes into focus, sharply and all of a sudden. "What did you say?"

She looks coolly at me. "I don't always tell people I'm neurodivergent."

The word is like a spell. "What does that mean?"

"It means 'having a different brain.' A different neurotype. Autistic, dyslexic, ADHD."

"Dyspraxic?" I blurt out, eyes wide and breath hitched.

"Yes," Opal concedes, her gaze perceptive and fixed on me with a knowing certainty. "Dyspraxia falls under 'neurodivergent.'"

I stare back at her. "You're like me?"

She stares back. "Well. I would hope you're doing better at school. Better than I did, at least."

"She is," Marley says, chuckling. Not quite picking up on the fact that I'm experiencing a slightly monumental moment here. Realizing I might not be the only person in my family who is different. "Ramya is super smart, it's only that she gives the teachers a lot of aggro. But she's one of Mr. Ishmael's favorites."

"I'm stuck in special workshops for kids with learning difficulties," I say irritably. "That's what they say I have. They say being dyspraxic is having a learning difficulty."

"Yes," Opal says gingerly. "Difficulty learning how to crush yourself down into a gray, artless cube. A lot of neurodivergent people have difficulty learning how to do that."

"Does my mum know?"

Both Leanna and Opal are slightly taken aback. "Know what?" asks Opal.

"That I'm . . ." I take a shuddering breath. "That you and I . . . that we're the same."

The two sisters exchange another wordless look.

"Yes," Opal eventually says quietly. "She does."

Angry, frustrated tears build.

"She saw how hard it was for me," Opal adds charitably. "She won't want that for you."

"But it's harder," I snap, my words lashing out like a coiled snake. "Feeling unsure and different without anyone understanding. Without anyone to go to. It makes it all harder."

"Your school doesn't help?" Leanna asks, concerned.

"They treat it as if it's something bad. Like I'm bad. Like it's something I have to unlearn."

Opal makes a small sound of derision. "Some things never change."

I'm aware that all my questions about witchcraft have vanished. This revelation, my first meeting with an adult who is like me, it's shaken me. It's woken me up. Quieted other parts. Ultimately left me with even more questions.

"Ramya." Opal speaks with the closest thing to a familial tone I've ever heard from her. "Being neuro-divergent. It's a good thing. But there's one thing I know neurodivergent people do a lot. Especially girls."

"Yeah?"

"Yes. That's try to right wrongs. Try to bring justice. I don't know why, maybe it's our wiring, but we can't be budged when it comes to doing the right thing."

I wait, prepared to be defensive.

"Ramya, I know you want to help people. You want to carry on your grandfather's work and make things better. But that's not your job."

I exhale sharply. "None of you get it. It is my job! I'm the one who can see through Glamour. I'm the one who can see what's happening. It's why he left me the book."

"And so what if he did?" Opal says bitterly. "You're not under any obligation to do anything with it. It's not your responsibility. Your only job, Ramya, is to have a childhood. A good one."

"I met a vampire whose father was killed because of a siren," I hiss, my temper firing up like a hot blue flame. "The Hidden Folk are scared. Fae are out prowling for me. Kelpies are losing members of their herd. This is serious. This is bad. I'm not going to bury my head and pretend there's nothing I can do when there's EVERYTHING I can do."

I wish they would just believe in me. I wish they would see what I'm trying to say.

"Mum and Dad took me on a skiing holiday once," I say. The room is so silent, my words seem to linger. "It was right after Mum cut ties with the family. Dad wanted to do lots of black runs, and Mum liked sitting in the lodge with mulled wine and magazines."

I remember the soft snow of the mountain. How heavy my feet felt with the skis.

"I would go on the chairlift a lot," I tell them. "Up the mountain, around the bend at the top, and down again. I liked the views. I liked the peace."

I remember the glorious feeling of the elevated bench taking off into the sky and carrying me away on a journey, high above the people skiing below.

"One time"—I flex my hands as I tell the story— "I slipped. Fell through the slight gap in the chairlift. I was hanging on with both of my hands and screaming like crazy."

Leanna gasps and Marley's mouth drops open. Opal watches me, giving nothing away.

"I screamed and screamed because I thought I was going to die," I say truthfully. "I thought I would lose my grip, fall, and the fall would be too far. There was such a cavern beneath my feet. I thought, No one is going to help me. No one will catch me. Then, suddenly, the chairlift ground to a halt. Someone had seen me and made them stop it. Then I heard all these people shouting from beneath me."

I still remember the feeling of staring down and seeing them. Their faint but earnest faces.

"They tore up parts of the netted fence," I continue, my voice trembling. "All of those people. Within seconds, they had made a huge net."

Take your skis off, little one. Someone had yelled that in a thick French accent.

"I kicked off my skis and I was so scared. But they were all yelling up in encouragement and telling me I was going to be okay."

So I let go. I dropped, trusting that they would take care of me.

"They caught me. All of them holding this net they had put together. Then they cheered and hugged me."

I laugh at the memory. The giddiness of it all. Mum running from the lodge in tears. The way one man ruffled my hair and one woman cupped my face, crying as hard as Mum.

"None of those people knew me," I say softly.

"But they didn't hesitate for a second. They jumped into action."

I wipe my eyes with my sleeve, turning my face away from the three of them for a moment.

"That's what people are. That's what we do. It's human nature to take care of each other. To help out. We're not mobs. We're not meant to be hateful. We're meant to help."

I look down at my hands. I rub the slight blisters I've developed from trying to use the rubber aids that the occupational therapist told me to get.

"If people aren't doing that, something's gone wrong. Something's not right. It's our natural instinct. So if we're turning on each other. If we're divided or tribal. Something is causing it. Something malevolent, something that's got to be stopped."

"Ramya," Leanna says softly, her eyes glistening. "That's so sweet. But—"

"No, no 'buts,' " I say wearily. "I'm going home. But that's why I'm finishing what Grandpa started. You have to accept it."

Something got in between our family. Something is making everything darker. Everyone more afraid. I'm not sitting by and doing nothing. I'm not letting them win, whoever they are.

Opal leaves while Marley and I do the dishes. Aunt Leanna keeps throwing me nervous glances, as if she is worried that I'll start bawling. I scrub each plate with ferocious intent. Marley is whistling, quite oblivious to my mood.

It's dark outside. I only have a few minutes before Aunt Leanna will take me home. I'm about to ask some more questions about Hidden Folk and witchcraft when we hear a loud, clear, and solitary knock on the shop door downstairs.

We all look to the front door of the flat, surprised that the sound carried so well.

"Is that Ren?" I ask, taking my rubber gloves off and shaking my hands.

"He has a key," Leanna says softly, her eyes still fixed upon the door.

Something unsettling has filled the room, like creeping smoke. We all continue to stare at the door, and each of us startles as another firm and resounding knock echoes up the stairs.

I move when they do not. Leanna speaks my name, but I race downstairs without looking back. The shop is in darkness, only the streetlamps from outside casting a sliver of light through the windows.

I stop dead at the foot of the stairs.

The two faeries from the Gruff Pub are peering through the glass panes of the shop door. When they spot me, their faces crack into devious sneers.

One puts a long, slender fingernail into the lock of the door and opens it.

Aunt Leanna and Marley clatter down the stairs to stand behind me. Aunt Leanna throws an arm around my cousin and stares at the faeries in very evident fright.

"The shop is closed, I'm afraid," she says, her voice quavering.

I know she cannot see the full horror of their unearthly appearance, but she can clearly sense their malevolence.

"We're not here to buy," one says, stepping inside. The one who broke the lock follows.

"Both of you, go upstairs," Aunt Leanna says loudly. "Now!"

The same faerie who broke the lock drags his long, jagged fingernail against the wooden counter that displays some of Aunt Leanna's wares. He cuts a long thin strip in the wood, causing all three of us to jump.

My eyes fall on the desk with the till and without thinking, I grab a glass paperweight. I brandish it like a weapon.

"One step closer and this is going straight at your head."

My aim is terrible, but they don't know that.

"Leave now," Aunt Leanna barks. "Or I'll call the police."

"What's going on in here?"

Everyone, including the faeries, turns to stare at

Ren, who is standing in the doorway looking bewildered. He looks to Leanna in confusion.

"You're back. Where's Opal? Who's this?"

The faeries exchange a glance and clearly communicate something silently. The one with the long nails steps away from the counter, and the other backs off.

"We were . . ." The first speaks silkily, but their words fade away, and I remember that they cannot tell lies. "We're leaving."

Ren nods firmly and watches them as they slink out of the shop. As soon as they're gone, he looks to Leanna in astonishment, and she lets out an enormous exhale.

"Thank God I came home when I did," Ren breathes, shocked. "Were they after the till money?"

"I suppose," Leanna says, sitting down on the steps and putting her head between her legs. "I just froze. Thank God you're here, Ren, you're right. Just in time."

She starts to cry, her shoulders shaking. Ren sits beside her and puts an arm around her.

"It's all right," he says soothingly. "Marley, go and put the kettle on."

Marley bolts up the stairs in obedience. I watch him go, my eyes narrowing.

"Forget them," Ren tells Leanna gently. "Put them out of your mind."

Aunt Leanna beams and a blissful expression crosses her face, at odds with the tears.

"You okay, Ramya?" Ren asks kindly, smiling up at me.

I realize that I'm still gripping the glass paperweight. Tightly.

"Yes," I say quietly, watching him, still chillingly aware that the fae are still out there somewhere. "I'm fine."

CHAPTER FIFTEEN

RADICAL

I'm wearing a purple beret today. I've ignored Marley's texts and gone for a walk around the Royal Mile on my own. I end up on West Nicolson Street, watching a couple of pigeons peck at a large pile of autumn leaves.

It's a very serene scene in October. Until one of the autumn leaves gets up and starts fighting back.

I shield my eyes from the cold sun and gape. When I look closer, I see it's no leaf. It's a very tiny creature with wings that resemble dead leaves, camouflaged brilliantly against a pile of autumn castaways.

Whatever it is, it battles the pigeon valiantly. The bird eventually flies away.

"Wait!" I call, before the creature can disappear as well.

It does not flee. Instead, it zooms toward me, seeming every bit as curious about me as I am about it.

Once it hovers in front of me, I can't help but release a noise of delight. It's a person with enormous wings and a tiny face, no bigger than an angel on top of a Christmas tree.

"You can see me?" she says, her skin glowing with pink undertones. She seems to be the first magical creature that is excited to be seen.

"What are you?" I instinctively hold out my palm, and the creature stands upon it.

"A sprite," she declares proudly, thumping her tiny sternum. Her wings twitch as she visibly inspects me. "What are you? Some kind of witch? You smell like one."

"Just a human," I say, my tone regretful. "You're what I thought the fae would look like."

The sprite sneezes in disgust and glares up at me, looking more adorable than aggressive. "Nasty, hateful things."

"Oh, I've seen some in the flesh," I assure her. "Not what the stories say."

"Vicious creatures." She shivers. "Are you the girl they're all talking about?"

"Probably," I laugh.

"You're starting a rebellion!"

"Oh!" I start at the word. "I don't know. Maybe."

I wonder what they're all saying about me. I

intend to stop sirens from haunting this city. I suppose that is a kind of rebellion to those who cannot help but fall under their spell.

"You're going to make it better," she gushes, smiling up at me. "The humans, they'll go back to how they were?"

I frown. "What do you mean?"

"They're very changed," she says sadly, her wings drooping as she does. "They lash out, they're far crueler than before. Can you change them back? Our nests are being destroyed and those who refuse to be spies have to go into hiding."

"Well." I bend down, gently returning her to the ground. "I'm not sure. I'm sort of on my own with all this."

The sprite cocks her head to one side, considering me. "You don't seem alone. They wouldn't be so afraid of you if you were."

I wince, not sure what to do with her words, but before I can say anything more, she soars away. I watch as her autumnal wings carry her far away and over the rooftops, out of sight. I think of Marley and Erica and Murrey.

Maybe the sprite is right. Maybe I'm not completely alone.

"Out for a walk?"

I leap to my feet, fists clenched and ready to swing. They relax when I see it's the Stranger, standing in the doorway of another bookshop. There's a black-and-white dog at his feet, panting and smiling in that way that only dogs can, with their tongues out.

"You a bookseller in this one, too?" I ask dryly.

"Just browsing," he replies cheerfully. "There's definitely something to interest you in here, though. Apart from the bookshop dog."

I look at the window displays. A sign saying it's a radical bookshop. "Seems a bit grown-up."

"Your loss," he says, shrugging. "Too bad. It's the one bookshop with your grandfather's only published work of nonfiction. As it's out of print, this is the only place to find a copy. Oh, well."

My blood seems to stop pumping and my legs are moving before my brain can catch up. I elbow past him and burst into the shop.

"Show me," I demand, once inside.

The Stranger's hand appears in front of my face, holding a small green paperback.

Witches, Warlocks, and Other Otherlings

BY JAMES STEWART-NAPIER

"He published a book!" I cry, flicking through the delicate pages.

"The book he left you is blank. It's for your

findings. Your discoveries. This book? This was his. His life's work."

I'm astonished. All this time, I thought it was his work I was undertaking. To be told that it's mine, my findings and my discoveries rather than his—it makes everything feel so much more significant. My cheeks are damp. My hands are unsteady. I remember what Murrey said. Connecting with someone through the words they leave behind.

"He was one of my favorite customers."

I look over at the bookseller. An elderly man with sparkling eyes and a deep emerald cardigan. He's wearing a boutonniere, knitted from bright wool.

"You knew my grandfather?" I ask, my voice shaking.

"He was a fixture of this city," the bookseller says warmly. "It's not the same place without him."

I flip open the green book.

While I cannot see or know the full reality of our magical brothers and sisters, I relish their existence and welcome them alongside me on this road of life. Anything that seeks to divide or monster us is not welcome in our community.

I try to picture him writing these words.

"When was this published?" I ask the bookseller, noticing that the Stranger is perusing the shelves.

"Five years ago, I think. Or thereabouts," the bookseller says thoughtfully.

"Five years, three months, and seventeen days," the Stranger says from the back of the shop, smiling at us with glinting teeth.

After Portia. After that night.

I turn some more pages.

"How's your own book coming along?"

I jump as the Stranger speaks, suddenly in front of me.

"Fine," I grumble. "I saw a sprite."

"See," he remarks placidly. "All sorts of things in this town once you start looking properly."

"What did he . . ." I pause, tucking my hair behind my ears and pulling the rim of my beret lower. "What did he say to you about me?"

"Nothing much, really," the Stranger muses. "Just that you were going to save everything."

My eyes wet and my teeth almost chatter. Such belief. Such expectation, from someone who is no longer here, it hits me like another arrow. I've become so comfortable with being tolerated. Teachers despair of me to the point of forgetting any potential I have. Mum and Dad are preoccupied with work and think academic achievement is the only measure of worth. I feel like, every day, I fail at being the person they all want me to be. Some nonexistent Ramya lives in their heads and whenever I don't behave as she would, I get the disappointed looks and the heavy sighs.

But Grandpa knew me. Knew the real Ramya. A neurodivergent girl who loves fashion and food and water, who can also see through Glamour.

He thought that was just fine. More than fine. He thought I could do something with it. Make the world better.

Maybe you don't need the whole world. Maybe you don't need a fridge full of gold stars. You don't need to fit the mold. You just need one person who believes you're right, just as you are. That the gifts you have, the way you're made, are enough to make something worthwhile of yourself.

"I'm coming back to buy this book," I tell the bookseller, my voice calm and resolute. "I am."

★

I CAN FEEL MARLEY GLANCING at me all through dinner. We're at Ren's house again. He's made really tasty sea bass and is telling a funny story about something that happened at the gallery. Aunt Leanna is laughing a little too hard. I listen, smiling in all the right places.

I can't fully explain why I'm distancing myself from Marley. Maybe I'm punishing him a tad for being such a goody-goody all the time. I know it's unkind of me, but I need some air. I need to do this on my own.

"How are your parents doing, Ramya?" Ren asks cordially.

I'm stumped by the question, but I suppose he's just very polite. "They're fine. They're working a bit later at the moment."

"Election next month," Aunt Leanna says. "Busy six weeks or so, then back to normal, I'm sure."

I shrug. I never know what it is they're covering on the television. It always seems boring and pointless.

"In fact, Ramya, I was wondering if I could have a word?"

I glance up, my mouth stuffed full of fish. I look to Aunt Leanna. Her expression is baffled.

"Everything all right?" she asks Ren.

"Oh, very all right," he says cheerfully. "Give us a minute, you two. Go walk for a bit."

Odd. I frown in confusion. A feeling that strengthens when Marley and Leanna get to their feet and start clearing their plates, smiling genially. They leave the room and I hear them clatter about in Ren's kitchen for a moment before heading out the back door and into the garden.

I turn back to Ren with a flicker of uneasiness. We sit across from each other in silence.

"Ramya, I was wondering if you could ask your parents something for me?"

I watch him carefully. "What would you like me to ask them?"

"Ask them to invite Leanna and me to your house for an evening. I'd love to talk more with them about their work."

I have to be careful here. Something has changed in the room. The air is different, the energy is altered.

"I'll ask them."

I say it quietly and without any kind of attitude. Just gentle assurance. It's obviously the correct thing to do, as Ren beams at me.

"Thank you, Ramya. I would really appreciate that."

When something is not entirely clear to me, I tell myself a story. I piece together what I know and let my instincts write the rest of the tale. I stare at Ren. I consider the story being presented.

"I read something really interesting about elephants today," I tell him abruptly, making my voice sound cheerful.

"Oh, yes?" he says blandly, smiling at me with cool indulgence. "What's that?"

"Some of them are evolving to be tuskless," I say smoothly. "They've been hounded by poachers and thieves for so long, they've learned to protect themselves by getting rid of the thing that made them a target."

"Hmm," Ren says, his gaze a touch less secure. "That is interesting."

"It's also sad," I add. "They had to hide something beautiful. They had to learn to conceal a part of what they are. All to avoid a predator. It's a hard life. Burying parts of yourself just so you can move more easily. Be a little safer."

Ren lets out a small laugh. "I confess, I don't think about the inner lives of elephants very often."

"Another cool thing about them," I go on, my voice hardening. "They're loyal to their families. They all look out for each other. And if anyone tries to hurt a member of the herd, they can be extremely dangerous."

Our eyes lock and it feels as if there is no room for breath in the dining room.

"Talk to your parents for me," Ren finally says, his words firm and pressing. "Soon."

He dabs his chin daintily with a linen napkin and then leaves the room, heading toward the garden. As I hear him call Leanna and Marley back in, I leap up and run to the front door.

I'm on the dock before I realize it. My knees are pressing down into the wooden pier, almost teetering over the edge. The sun is nearly down, and the water is as black and murky as the water in the art classroom once all the paint has been washed inside it.

I reach one hand down and sink it slowly into the depths, marveling at the cold contact.

"Are you here?" I whisper.

A long stretch of time goes by. Nothing happens. My hand is starting to numb inside the water.

"Come on." My voice cracks. "Come back, come on."

"Ramya!"

Aunt Leanna is calling my name from Ren's front doorway.

"Ramya, get away from the water."

I snatch my hand back, swearing softly. I stagger to my feet and turn. My aunt is peering in bemusement, gesturing for me to come back inside the house.

I go. Slowly.

As I pass Ren's boat floating by the pier, I turn back to look out at the Forth.

There I see them. One of them. His ears and eyes just above the surface of the water, watching. Waiting.

I hold his gaze for a moment.

The kelpie exhales through his large nostrils, a spray of water hitting the gentle wave of the river.

"What are you looking at?" murmurs Leanna, coming to stand beside me.

She cannot see them. Just like Marley. Just like everyone else.

"Nothing," I tell her softly.

The kelpie's head disappears beneath the depths, leaving me to stare at the black water.

CHAPTER SIXTEEN

A WITCH HUNT

"What's up with you?"

Marley asks the question from behind as I approach the door to the real Grassmarket.

"Nothing," I say stiffly. "I'm going down."

"I'm coming with you."

I exhale despairingly. "You can't even see this door."

"I don't need to see it in order to use it."

"Fine. But don't slow me down."

"Stop being mean."

"Stop being needy."

He starts to retort to that, but I kick open the door next to the drinking fountain and pull him inside after me. He falls instantly silent once we're alone in the dark. I get out the flashlight I stole from Dad's toolbox and shove it into Marley's hands.

He clicks it on and gasps when he lays eyes on the dark, dangling staircase.

"Don't lose your nerve or your footing," I whisper as I start to descend.

Marley climbs down behind me, slowly and deliberately. Neither of us speaks. Me because it takes every bit of my concentration to avoid slipping. Marley because he's taking it all in.

When we reach the market door at the bottom of the stairs, I turn to my cousin.

"There's no Glamour down here."

Marley's eyes widen. "What?"

"It's their safe space. Their underground layer. None of the Hidden Folk will wear Glamour. So don't stare too much. We're guests down here."

He swallows but nods. I nod back.

As I open the door, blasting both of us with vibrant colors and new sounds and smells, I take a small degree of pleasure in watching Marley's reaction. His eyes absorb the high ceiling, all the marvelous stalls, the distinct assortment of vendors and the small creatures skipping about.

"This is . . ."

His words fade away as a small green dragon,

made of paper, lands jauntily by a sconce on the wall. It puffs and blows out a small breath of fire, lighting the sconce with a miniature flame.

"Wow!" Marley exclaims, expressing the wonder and amazement I felt when first seeing the market.

"Come and see what they're selling," I say.

We move to a stall manned by a male troll. He is tall, with ears that stick out like handles on a water jug. Marley registers his appearance with a great deal of surprise and apprehension.

"What's selling?" I ask the troll.

"Some lovely yellow today," the troll says merrily. "Line the inside of your shoes with it and you'll never have cold feet. Very popular with brides-to-be."

I arch an eyebrow. "We're children."

Marley laughs and reaches out to touch the vivid wares for sale.

"Do you have anything that would protect someone from a siren?" I ask bluntly.

The troll glances around nervously and speaks in a hushed tone. "Not today, no. If I had some terracotta, you could put that in your pocket to ward off bad influences. Only for a day or so."

"A day is better than nothing," I murmur. "What would that cost?"

"With the way things are at the moment, it's pretty in demand."

"I bet."

We move away from the troll's wares and continue down the long hall. A pair of sprites hum right by us and sit gleefully on a beam over our heads. One has wings like a cobweb, the other like a butterfly.

I spot Freddy peering at a stall in the corner. "That's Freddy. The boy I told you about."

"The one you said was pretty?"

"Shut up."

"Your boyfriend, Freddy?"

I glower at him.

"Must be half-term for him as well," I say. "And he's not my boyfriend!"

"What's he lurking around here for?"

"Same as us, I imagine."

Two small creatures, no taller than tree stumps, are seated on stools just up ahead. They look like gnomes, but instead of white hair, their beards are made of bark. They're playing a game with dice. Only it's dice I've never seen before, with eight sides instead of six. Marley and I are quite enthralled by their game. So enthralled, we both squeak in surprise when long fingers with sharp nails grip our shoulders from behind.

"How nice of the humans to come all the way down here to visit us."

Faerie.

She towers over us, taller than any human I've

met. Her skin is so pale, the veins stand out. Only they aren't blue like human blood beneath the skin, but deep purple. Her eyes are fiendish, and when I look into them, I can see large, shining white circles that take up the whole iris. The white circles glow, almost hypnotically.

Marley makes a sound of distress, and I suddenly realize we're being moved into one of the alcoves. I turn my head just in time to catch Freddy Melville's eye before the faerie pushes away a velvet curtain in the booth, revealing a long corridor.

The creature does not speak as she propels us down the corridor. We're steered into a small room with no furnishings or windows, only one lit sconce on the wall. The room is dim, and Marley and I back up against the wall as the faerie closes the door behind us.

I remember what Marley told me of the fae. That they can be devious and wicked but are incapable of lying. They can also sniff out lies in other people. If we're going to get out of here unscathed, I'm going to have to talk like a politician and avoid giving direct answers.

"His mother and my aunt know we're together," I say. The truth.

The faerie laughs. It's a high-pitched, chilling sound.

"Do they know you're down here?"

I fumble. A direct question, one that tells us she knows we're here without any adults knowing.

"Oh, dear," she says, delighted. "I don't think so."

"What do you want?" I snap, putting as much ferocity into my voice as I can, in an attempt to sound less afraid.

"You have no business being in our shadows," the faerie says in velvet tones. "What are you searching for?"

I can't think of an answer I like, so I stay silent. The faerie considers us and then reaches forward, taking my leopard-print beret from my head. She puts it slowly onto her own. It looks almost comical against the iron-straight white hair.

"I was showing my cousin the market," I say. Not a lie.

"What"—the faerie leans right into my face, her jagged teeth and bright eyes too close to be comfortable—"are you searching for?"

From a distance, the fae seemed almost perfect. Beautiful in an ethereal, untouchable way. Up close they seem rotten. Physically perfect but radiating cruelty.

"I'm looking for a witch." I say it boldly, staring into the bright white circles in the faerie's eyes.

"Ramya," Marley whispers, but I don't turn away from the faerie.

She stares at me with an expression of amusement. Yet there's something darker underneath it. Something full of hate and animosity and rage. Barely contained fury.

"What are you?" the faerie finally says, her voice dangerously soft. "At first, when I heard you were scampering around the city searching for things to play with, I thought you were just some fool with a death wish."

"I'm not looking for things to play with," I reply icily. "I'm letting people tell me their stories."

That high-pitched laugh once again. "Tell you their stories? How revolting."

"The kelpie that went missing," I snap, wanting to wipe the pitilessly smug expression off the faerie's face. "They will have had a story."

"Oh, to be sure," muses the faerie. She runs one long nail down my face, making me flinch. "She was fun to play with. They're not so intimidating once you drag them out of the water."

I'm as cold as the river water the kelpies inhabit. My ears feel momentarily blocked. It must be a cruel lie. A nasty attempt to upset and frighten us.

But they cannot lie.

"Why would you do something like that?"

It's Marley who has spoken, not me. I'm proud of him. Unable to speak myself, too horrified by this creature and the menace radiating from her. Marley stares up at her with indignation. It's the most withering expression I've ever seen him wear. I look to the faerie, expecting to see a glimmer of shame or remorse.

Instead, she is hungry. As if our outrage, our pain, is feeding her.

"I did it because I could," she says, savoring every word. "And because I wanted to."

I want to hit her. Her cold ferocity and the way she's proudly bragging about hurting another being are so infuriating, I want to smack the smirk right from her face. She must sense it because she's staring at me now, with a challenge in her quick eyes.

She wants me to do it. So I don't.

"What are you going to do to us?" Marley snaps, squaring up to the faerie. Standing right at my side.

"You," she says slowly, pointing at Marley. "As much as I'd love to make an oubliette for you and see how long it takes you to crack, you have a whole storm of people around you. I can sense them. They would miss you. Very messy."

She's not wrong. Aunt Leanna. Ren. Gran. Half the teachers at school. Aunt Opal. They would all notice the moment Marley didn't come home, and I doubt even the fae would be safe from their combined wrath.

"But you," she says malevolently as her finger snaps from pointing at Marley to pointing at me.

Her serrated teeth grimace in a demonic smile. Her eyes are ravenous. "I don't think anyone cares about you. I doubt anyone would come looking."

It's a quick and seamless knife in the side. Slid in and out without ceremony. My whole jaw trembles as I use every muscle I have to lock down my emotions, not wanting her to see just how well she landed the blow.

"Search for that witch all you like," she adds. "I'm sure she's a great deal smarter than you. I'm sure she knows it's wise to stay hidden and out of our business. This town doesn't need a sheriff throwing their weight around."

"You're afraid of her," I say softly, channeling all my hurt and despair into the words. "Whoever she is, you're scared."

The faerie recoils with a sneer.

"You're contributing to the dark cloud coming down on Edinburgh," I say accusingly. "Hurting kelpies, scaring people. I hear you've been asking about me around town. Do I scare you too?"

Another cruel laugh. Then suddenly, her hands are around my neck. I sputter and gasp and her hands tighten ever so slightly.

"Let her go!" yelps Marley, kicking the faerie hard.

She lets go, momentarily ready to strike my cousin down. Then something distracts her.

Water. The room is slowly but steadily filling up with water. I glance down, almost absentmindedly, and stare as my feet become engulfed in cold water.

The faerie hisses and spits, seeming feral at the touch of it. Her eyes snap to mine and every inch of her is vibrating with rage.

"What. Are. You?"

I can't understand why she's relating any of this to me, but the water is starting to fill up the room. The door is wedged open with great effort and Freddy appears in the frame.

"Come on!" he yells to the two of us.

Marley splashes over to him, wading in the now knee-high water. I shake myself out of my nearly catatonic state and move to follow him.

The faerie grabs me. "You're lucky Lavrentiy wants to deal with you."

I glower. "Who?"

"If you find your witch," she hisses, her nails digging into my arm, "tell her to stay hidden. Just like the rest of us. Or it's going to get bad out there."

I wrench myself free. "It's already bad out there. I am going to find her. Wherever she is."

She sneers as I shove myself free and wade toward the doorway. "Oh, really? And then what?"

"Try me and find out!"

She'll know what to do. This powerful witch that they're all so afraid of, she'll have all the answers when I only have questions. By finding her, I find the key to wiping the smirks off their faces. To ending Erica's fear. To making Hidden Folk like Murrey and the sprite feel safer. By finding her, I end this nasty, tumultuous period of unease because she will know how to finish it.

Another wave of water appears inside the room, causing the faerie to push me aside and flee. I feel Marley and Freddy grab onto me and drag me along the corridor toward the exit. I'm a little unsteady on my feet but by the time we reach the underground market square, I'm calmer.

I stop. I crouch over and take a few deep breaths.

"What," Marley cries, shaking the wet bottoms of his jeans, "was that?"

"That was her," I say, and I can hear the delight and relief in my voice. "That was her. That was the witch. The one who's going to help us."

CHAPTER SEVENTEEN

SUBSTITUTE

I come down to breakfast at home, weighed down with secrets and memories of the water flooding in and the cruelty of the faerie, and instantly sense something is wrong.

Mum and Dad are standing, in their work clothes, by the fridge. They're both feverishly scrolling through their phones.

"What's the problem?" I ask.

"Lydia's mum has had a stroke," Mum says, her voice full of frustration and not one drop of sympathy. "She can't watch you today."

"That's fine, I'll hang out around town."

"No," Mum says sharply. Then she forces herself to calm down. "Sorry. No. Dad and I would rather you didn't. We don't want you to do that anymore."

"But you're always saying how safe Edinburgh is."

"It was," Mum says softly. "At one time, it was."

"Then I'll go and stay with Leanna at the shop."

"We've been trying to call her all morning," Dad says, glancing at the clock on the wall, at the timer on the oven, and then at his Rolex. He frowns at all three and then dials what I assume is Aunt Leanna's number again. "It's ringing out, Cass!"

"Fine," Mum says flatly. "Then—"

"No!" Dad interjects before she can even hint at whatever it was she was going to say. "No. I'd rather we call your mother."

"Oh, sure," Mum says snappily. "Only a quick four-and-a-half-hour drive down from Loch Ness— she'll be here in a jiff."

"She could come on her broomstick," Dad mutters.

"Oh, nice, Mike!"

"What!" Dad feigns complete innocence and then huffs out a breath. "Right. I'll ask the neighbors."

He won't. The ones on the left are a bunch of trust fund babies who have parties late into the night, and the ones on the right packed up for Portugal two days ago and won't be back until November.

I see this thought pass over both of my parents' faces.

"I'm calling her," Mum says steadily. "Or Rams comes to work with us."

Dad sighs bitterly. "Fine."

Twenty minutes later, we're all sitting at the breakfast bar when the doorbell rings. Dad mutters something incoherent but Mum leaps up and runs to answer it.

She and Aunt Opal just stare at each other for a moment.

Mum is wearing an expensive blouse and tailored trousers that she buys with a special allowance from her work. Opal is wearing a miniskirt, ripped tights, and a leather jacket that says **GIRL POWER** in massive bubble-gum writing.

"Thank you," Mum finally says laboriously. "For doing this on such short notice."

"It's fine," Opal replies smoothly. "Family."

Mum suddenly realizes that she's blocking the door and jumps to one side, gesturing for Opal to come in. "Do you need some money or—"

"No," Opal interrupts, giving her a reproving glance. "I don't need money."

She saunters inside and joins Dad and me in the kitchen. Dad watches her with so much distrust, as if she were a stray cat that wandered in with a bird in its mouth.

"I can take it from here," Opal tells him. "Go. Read the headlines, tell people who to vote for, and who to be scared of, all that good stuff."

Dad scowls, but Mum makes a noise that says,

"Let it go." They grab their things and head out to the car. Dad throws one last reproachful look at Opal, and Mum tells us to phone if there are any problems.

Then it's just the two of us in the house.

Opal moves to the fridge and takes out a carton of tomato juice. She finds a tall glass and fills it with ice, then pours the thick red liquid over it.

"Do you know where your mum keeps her hot sauce?" she asks.

"Spice cupboard," I say, nodding to the wall of cabinets behind her.

"Nice and strong," she says, examining the label. "Your mum always did love a bit of fire."

She lets a few drops of hot sauce fall into the glass, then adds salt and pepper. I watch as she cuts up a lemon from Mum's fruit bowl. As she squeezes some juice into the glass, she looks up at me. "You hungry?"

"No," I tell her. "What are you making?"

"An early-morning potion."

"I saw her."

"Saw whom?"

"The Heartbroken Witch."

Opal raises one eyebrow perfectly and regards me coolly. "Oh, really?"

"Well." I correct myself. "I didn't actually *see* her. But she got us out of a slightly hairy situation."

Opal takes a long, slow sip of her red concoction. "Did the hairy situation happen upon the two of you while you were at the library, doing your homework and minding your own business?"

I roll my eyes. "No. But there's a vampire at the library, it's not completely safe either."

Not that Murrey would hurt anyone.

"So," Opal goes on. "You were both somewhere you were not supposed to be, doing something I've specifically told you not to do, and then what happened?"

"We had an unfortunate run-in with the fae."

Opal's slightly bored expression sharpens into one of horrified concern. "What?"

"Yeah."

"Ramya, that's not funny."

"I know!" I say indignantly. "Believe me, I did not see the funny side."

"All right," Opal says, clearly keeping a lid on her temper. "What happened?"

"We were in the Grassmarket and one of them grabbed us. She was trying to scare me out of hunting for the witch—"

"Good," snaps Opal. "I have no idea what you're expecting to find, or what you want this witch to do. I'm not even sure you do."

"The faerie was scared of her," I say triumphantly. "She got all fidgety when I mentioned I was searching for a witch. The kelpies believe in her. If she comes out of hiding, maybe the fae and the sirens will stop."

"They'll never stop," murmurs Opal, turning away from me to wash her glass.

"The faerie hurt one of the kelpies. For sport. They'll do worse to other Hidden Folk; everyone is afraid of them. We just need one person to stand up to them, and for everyone else who—"

"You've been reading too many stories," Opal says quietly. "People will always do bad things for power. You're placing all this expectation on someone you don't even know."

"But she saved us!" I retort, slamming my hands down on the breakfast bar. "The faerie was keeping us in this tiny, dark room and when I thought things were about to get really bad, the room started filling up with water."

Opal stops washing the glass. Her shoulders stiffen. Then she turns, her eyes wide and full of incredulity. "That's not possible."

"It did! You can ask Marley! You can ask anyone in the market; we ran out of there drenched."

"There was no one there to cast such a spell," Opal says, more to herself than me. "Was there?"

"Well, we couldn't see her. But who else could it be? Another witch?"

Opal watches me carefully. "Perhaps."

"Well, anyway," I say. "She saved us. She was watching out for us. We're not alone. I just need to find her and then we can work out what to do."

"What are you talking about?" she breathes despairingly.

"Grandpa wanted me to meet Hidden Folk. He wanted me to get to know them. He wanted me to be a part of that community. And now that community is in danger."

"Your community is aboveground," Opal says starkly. "In the light. At school. Here. With humans."

"No!" I bark, pushing myself away from my chair and glaring at her. "I've never had a community. I've never even had friends. I don't know how you can stand there and act like you don't know what I'm talking about. You're. Like. Me."

She watches me, completely still.

"You're autistic. Mum told me when I pressed her. But we're alike. Our brains, they're different neurotypes. We're not like most people. Don't stand there and say I have a community, I don't! I've got a lifetime of 'You're doing it wrong' and 'Why are you so different?' I've got, 'Oh, Ramya, don't you mean dyslexia? You're dyslexic.' No, I mean dyspraxic, and it doesn't give people the right to treat me like I'm a freak. I'm smarter than all of them, it's only that I process at a different speed. I'm so sick of having to slow down for everyone when they need to go at their pace, but then the minute I need people to be patient, it's completely impossible. Suddenly, I'm the one with difficulties, I'm the one who has to go through hours of workshops. I'm sick of idiots saying 'Oh, Ramya, focus on ability, not disability.' I'm sick of the positive mental attitude rubbish. I'm sick of it because ninety percent of what makes life harder comes from them, not me!"

I'm out of breath, anger crackling through me like an electric cable.

"I'm finally doing something that feels right," I add desperately. "I finally feel like I fit somewhere. I have a purpose. I know what I'm supposed to do."

I feel my shoulders drop as I stare up at her.

"Don't take this away from me," I finally say quietly. "It's all I have left of him."

I can't be sure but, for one brief moment, I think I see understanding in her face. Then she turns away, moving to the counter to pick up the kitchen television remote. She switches it on and then punches in a channel number, one in the two hundreds.

It's a live broadcast of a massive chamber in an old building.

"What is it?" I ask, baffled.

She waits and when the camera cuts to a cluster of people sitting on a long bench, she pauses the remote. The screen freezes.

"Do you recognize any of them?" she asks, using the remote to point to the screen.

I look closely. Then let out a gargled sound.

It's her. Portia. She's listening to someone in the chamber giving a speech, seeming bored.

"It's her," I croak, getting right up to the screen. "The siren."

Opal switches off the television, satisfied. "Let's just say she's getting more powerful."

I feel slightly sick. That face, it was exactly as I remembered. While I can never hold an image of the Stranger in my mind, hers has never left.

"That's what sirens do," Opal says distantly. "They slither into powerful places and make their home there. They whisper in the ears of important people. They act for themselves alone."

"You've met one?" I ask.

"One or two."

"Did their voices work on you—"

"Ramya, I'm not telling you to stay away from sirens to be mean. I'm not trying to rain on your parade. I just know it never ends well. Dad spent years hearing sob stories from Hidden Folk about how sirens were making life harder and look what happened."

I frown. "He was sick. In the end, he was ill?"

Her face flickers but then the mask reappears. Calm. Assured. "Yes. In the end. But his whole life was about an obsession with sirens and Hidden Folk. When it should have been about . . . other things."

"But Grandpa wasn't immune like me," I say. "They don't work on me, Aunt Opal."

She exhales but then smiles reluctantly. "That is certainly a good thing."

We don't speak for a moment. A blackbird is singing outside. I can hear the steady tip-tap of the laundry room leak starting up again. I turn back to Opal and find her staring at my hands. She nods toward them when she catches me.

"Your hands need certain stimulation because you're dyspraxic."

I glance down at them. It's true, I often feel the desperate need to squeeze something or to flex. It's like there are marbles inside my palms and I have to keep them moving and stretching to stop any heaviness.

"I'll tell Cass to get you some stim toys."

I flex my palms and nod, surprised. "Thank you."

She nods back and we don't say anything more.

She is still regarding my hands with a thoughtful expression.

And the leak continues to drip.

CHAPTER EIGHTEEN

LAVRENTIY

It's the Sunday before our half-term is over and I'm standing on the doorstep of Aunt Leanna's shop. I slipped away from Lydia and it's raining very lightly as I pound on the door. Something just doesn't sit right about the other day. Aunt Leanna letting her phone ring and ring, it isn't like her. Marley isn't answering my texts, either.

My hand starts to hurt, so I stop to give my knuckles a quick massage. I'm about to knock again when the door is pried open.

Marley is in front of me, regarding me like I'm a maniac.

"There you are!" I say in exasperation. "What's going on, where've you been?"

"Here," Marley answers, but he doesn't sound like himself. "Where else would we be?"

"My parents were calling Leanna again and again yesterday," I say. "I had to sneak away today."

"Mum was doing accounts yesterday," he replies dully. "She was busy."

"All right," I mutter, a little defensively. "I'm going back to the water to talk to the kelpies—you coming?"

"Not today, Ramya."

I jump at the sound of a third voice. Ren is suddenly standing behind Marley, in the dark interior of the shop. He's smiling serenely at me, but his eyes are cold.

"Oh," I say.

"Did you get a moment to ask your parents?" Ren speaks with soft menace. "About what we discussed?"

I have a choice in this moment. I could play along and say I did and they're considering it or waiting for the right moment. A small survival instinct inside me is begging me to do just that. To fob off his question and make up some lie.

But I can't. Not if I'm listening to my instincts. To my gut, my core. To the part of me that stood ramrod straight all those years ago at the sound of Portia's voice. I was so unaffected back then. Just pure intuition. Hard to fool, difficult to sway. My gift working like a charm to protect me from them. I knew when something was wrong because everything inside me would line up.

It's lining up now.

"I'd like to speak to my cousin, please, Ren," I say in a low voice. "Now."

Ren looks upon me with a passive expression. He seems unfazed but there is a flint of curiosity bright and alive in his eyes.

"Tell me why," he says. A command. Simple and clear. I can feel the waves of compulsion in his voice as they hit the back of Marley's head, causing him to glare at me.

This man, whom Leanna and Marley adore. So genial, so giving. The man who smiles all the time. Someone who moves with such grace and ease, seemingly making everyone else do the same.

I raise my chin, acknowledging that I heard his command. "No."

It's almost like a wind sweeps through the room, from the back of Leanna's shop and out the doorway. A cold, clamoring wind that hits me in my bones and makes my lungs turn to ice.

"Very interesting, Ramya," Ren says, the words almost inaudible. "Very interesting indeed. Marley. You have five minutes."

Marley stumbles out onto the street, scowling at me. The door shuts with a dainty snick behind him.

"He's one of them," I say brokenly. "You know that, right?"

Marley shakes his head slowly. "You're unbelievable."

I look at my cousin with a watchful gaze. He's being influenced by Ren, I'm sure of it. "Why?"

He glares at me. "You're envious."

"No, Marley," I say quietly. "I'm not."

"You are. You're upset because Ren cares about me and Mum, and your parents barely know you're alive."

I bite my cheeks. Hard. "That's not nice."

"Well, it's true!" Marley snaps, his eyes full of frenzy and anger. "The faerie wasn't wrong, Ramya. There's a reason no one cares that you're trapsing around town."

A single tear rolls down my face, landing on the cobblestones beneath our feet. "This isn't you saying this."

"Yes, it is. I'm tired of running around after you. You're jealous of my family because I actually have one. Ren, Mum, Gran. And Grandpa."

"He was my family too," I say, desperately trying to keep my composure.

"No, he wasn't. You were off in London. You should go back there. Go back to where you came from and stop bothering us."

"Go back to where I came from?" I repeat incredulously. "Marley, that's disgusting. You don't say things like that. You never say things like that to anyone."

"You're accusing Ren of being one of those horrible things," Marley retorts fiercely. "Not that I think they actually exist. I think you've made it up in your head."

"You're out here saying awful things because you think he needs defending," I tell him sharply. "This is classic behavior. You're acting just like Mum and Dad did that night with Grandpa and Portia."

"I'm not acting like anything. Maybe I'm just tired of you bossing me around and telling me what to do. Ren is actually nice to me, Ramya."

I feel a modicum of shame, and desperation creeps into my voice. "He's a rat, Marley. You're behaving as though you're under a spell."

"Well, maybe that's because I don't like you very much," he says. "Same as them."

While the cruel words of the faerie made me feel as if I were being stabbed, this is so much worse. Like force-fed poison.

"Get away from me," I say wretchedly. "Go back to your siren. He's trying to rip your family apart, like she did mine, but go on. Let it happen."

I turn around and storm away, waiting until I

hear him go back into the shop before I let go and bawl. I double over and hug myself. I sob and gasp and let the salty tears fall away from me. Trying to get the poison out.

★

"YOU LOOK AWFUL."

I'm in the Grassmarket. If Lydia is out searching for me, she'll never find me here. No one will. I alone can see through the Glamour, me and the Hidden Folk. It's probably dark out by now but I'm underground and away from the light.

But no one is looking for me. I know that now.

"Thank you," I tell the vendor sarcastically.

The troll manning the stall gives me a sympathetic look. "I only meant you seem a bit out of sorts."

"Do you have any straw that will make you forget things?" I ask hoarsely.

The troll gives me a sad look. "No. Not that I would sell to you."

I wipe my nose so harshly that my beret is almost dislodged. I balance it more gracefully on top of my head. "Why not?"

"Never sell forget-mes or forget-me-nots to someone in an emotional state. Magic is always better with a clear head and an unbroken heart. I always say, when magic is blue, it's not for you."

I step away from the stall, furious at the new layer of tears starting to brim. I walk over to a booth and sit down. I take Grandpa's book out of my bag and place it carefully in front of me.

I flip through it, rereading the notes I've been making.

A vampire named Murrey, a Hulder named Erica. A sprite with autumnal wings. The fae. A poor drawing of the two little gnomes playing their game of dice. The troll working as a stall vendor. I went from thinking that the world could only ever be a place for one kind of story to discovering a whole host of realities I never knew were possible. I was always selfish in believing that I was the only person who truly understood what it felt like to be different.

The Hidden Folk were all around me, magnificent in their difference, and I was too stubborn to see it.

"Witchcraft is like singing," I murmur, tracing some of my notes. "Some are born able to hit a high C. Others work at it. Some never have what it takes at all."

No Heartbroken Witch. No witch at all. Wherever she is, she's not coming to help us. I can see that now.

I take out the business card and curse when I see it's blank.

"Help me," I plead, shaking it. "I need you now, help me!"

Nothing. It remains blank. I shake it. I am tempted to rip it apart. I throw it across the table only to snatch it back and crumple it up in my fist.

I don't know how I got here. I wanted to help, I wanted to be the hero for once in my life. Instead I have no instructions, everyone is in greater danger than ever, and I don't know what to do.

I flip the book open to the back page, meaning to stick the card there, when I notice something. Writing starts to form and appear across the page, just as it did when I first opened the book.

Dear Ramya,

I almost leap away from it. I'm shaking. I know the words aren't actually being written by an invisible hand, but it feels that way.

I know if you're reading this, something has happened. I can't say what. I've made the odd enemy around town since trying to unite the Hidden Folk. Something I know you will be better at than me.

My eyes are hurting. My chest is too tight, like someone has me tied up and they're pulling too hard on the rope.

But I need you to know, Ramya. I'm well aware of what a sacrifice this is. What it asks of you. I don't believe in the Chosen One. There never is a Chosen One. No such thing exists. Only someone who chooses to do the right thing, and those who choose to follow them.

I sniff, fiercely. Desperately.

It's all right to refuse. It's all right to walk away. It's all right to go home. I promise it is. I know how strong and brave and incredible you are. But that doesn't mean you have to sacrifice any of it.

I wait for more to appear, but nothing does. I stare at the words, completely astounded.

"Ramya?"

I jerk at the sound of my name. It's Freddy Melville. In faded jeans and a school sweater, one that tells me he goes to the posh all-boys school not far from ours. I glance up at him sadly and then look away.

"Are you all right?" he asks awkwardly, tapping my foot with his toe.

"No," I say honestly. "I'd rather be alone."

Not true, but I don't have the energy to put a mask on.

Maybe masking, pretending to be just like everybody else, is what it feels like to wear Glamour. No wonder the Hidden Folk come here to escape that. To be exactly as they are, free from hiding. Free from suppressing parts of themselves to be safe.

Maybe I knew what that felt like all along.

"I saw your cousin getting into a car," Freddy says urgently. "I watched them drive off. It didn't look good."

"He's fine," I say bitterly. "Probably going for an evening drive with his dream would-be stepfather. Who is a siren, by the by."

"It was a man driving," concedes Freddy, sitting across from me. "It didn't seem cordial, though. In fact, Marley was really upset."

"Where was my aunt?"

"Not there."

Something is not right.

"It's not my business," I say resentfully. "He's made that perfectly clear."

Freddy stares down at his hands. He seems really nervous.

"What?" I ask. "What is it?"

"Ramya, there's something you need to know."

I'm so tired. Bone-tired. Exhausted like I've been trying to run up and over a wall. The enthusiasm I felt during the initial attempts is gone, and so is the determination that followed that. Now I'm left with fatigue and bruises. Completely prepared to give up.

"I think your cousin is probably in danger."

"That's what I need to know? I doubt it. What would Ren have to gain from hurting Marley?"

"It's not always about gain with sirens," Freddy says quietly. "It's sport for them."

"If he hurt Marley, the police would find out. They would do something."

"Oh, yeah? You don't think a siren can talk their way out of a police cell?"

I frown, starting to feel very uneasy. "Why are you—"

"I know what sirens can do, Ramya," Freddy says, his voice a frantic mixture of resolve and restlessness. "Okay, I know them. Really well. I don't just know what they're capable of, I know who they are. Lavrentiy is one of the older ones. He's dangerous. If that's Marley's stepfather, this is not going to end well."

"Lavrentiy." I test out the name. "Ren. You think that's him?"

Then I remember the faerie using that name. The memory sends ice through my head.

"You really think Marley's in trouble?"

"If what I've always heard about Lavrentiy is true, then yes. I do."

"He wanted to get close to my parents," I say absentmindedly. "They're news anchors."

Freddy makes a noise of derision. "Figures. Access to television would give him tons more power."

"That's why?" I look at him. "He wanted to be on television."

"On it? Unlikely. Behind what's broadcast? Very possibly."

I shudder. "So why take Marley?"

I feel myself getting to my feet as I ask the question, heading toward the other side of the market. The exit. Freddy follows me.

"Ramya, you need to know—"

"Where's your little sidekick?"

Both Freddy and I turn. The faerie is leaning against a dark corner of an alcove, watching us with sinister fascination.

"He's with Lavrentiy," I say coldly. "What do you know about it?"

"Only that he probably won't come back."

I lunge at her, but Freddy grabs me.

"Leave." Freddy tells the faerie. "Don't bother us."

The faerie arches an eyebrow at the command but, to my shock, obeys. I watch her slope away without comment and then I turn to Freddy, whose hands are still gripping my shoulders.

"You," I say, horror-struck. "You!"

"I wanted to tell you," he says gently. "It's a hard thing to admit."

I wrestle free and stumble backward, away from him. "You're one of them?"

He looks back at me like he's in pain. "Yes. And no. I'm not like the others. I have the power. I don't use it unless I must."

"Erica." I say the Hulder's name, remembering our first meeting right here in this very market. "Does she know?"

"No," he says softly. "Ramya, I know you won't trust me, but I want to help. I don't agree with Ren or the fae. I don't like the stories I've been hearing. Hidden Folk terrorized, creatures going missing. I don't like any of it. And now they're trying to fracture the human world . . . I want no part in it. I want to stop it."

He sounds like me. Not so long ago.

"Ramya, you're powerful," he says fiercely. "You are. Everything changed when you got here and started asking questions. Whispers, rumors. About a human who can see through us all. But who still wants to help us. We can work together and make the one thing that will beat creatures like Ren."

"And what's that?"

"Community!" Freddy says earnestly. "Friendship! The one thing sirens and fae generally cannot do is work together. They can't stand camaraderie;

they would betray each other without a second thought. They're not loyal."

"Then how can I trust you?"

"Because I'm not like other sirens," he says softly. "Just like you're not like other humans."

We stand there staring at each other. Two misfits without a community.

"I'm not your enemy," he says at last. "I promise."

He saved us from that faerie. He helped me with my notes.

I suppose I should decide who my enemies are based on what they do, rather than what they are.

"I need to save my cousin," I say forcefully. "Are you in?"

He holds out his hand for me to shake. "All in."

I shake it with feeling. "Then we need to go."

"What about an adult?"

I laugh bitterly and then do something impulsive. I climb up onto one of the stalls, ignoring the objections from its vendor.

"This is a message for the Heartbroken Witch!" I shout, causing the whole market to fall quiet and listen to me. "Tell her we need her back. Tell her we're running out of time. Tell her she can find me on Inchkeith island."

"Ramya!"

I see Murrey in the crowd, his face full of worry as he calls my name.

"Will anyone come with me?" I call out, my voice shaking. "A siren has my cousin. Who will help me?"

Murrey's eyes fall. A few Hidden Folk turn away so I cannot read their expressions. Erica steps forward from the back of the room.

"Ramya," she says softly, apologetically. "If any of us stand up to a siren, we'll be killed. That's what they do. That's what they want, they want you to put yourself in danger."

"They have my cousin," I say flatly, staring back at her. Disappointment edging into my words. "I don't have a choice, I'm going. I'm only asking if I'm going alone."

More downcast gazes.

"Fine," I say brokenly. "Tell the witch I'm not hiding anymore. I'm not afraid."

I've never been so afraid.

My heart almost stops as I spot a familiar face at the back. The Stranger. He lowers a newspaper to regard me, something odd and unreadable in his expression.

"Tell her I'm done waiting," I call, glaring right at him. "I'm doing this with or without her."

I leap back down and head for the exit, ignoring the spluttering and confused murmuring that I leave behind. Freddy is on my heels as I rush up the stairs. I occasionally stumble but it doesn't slow me down.

"Inchkeith island?" Freddy calls up to me as we near the door. "Why there?"

"Marley always wanted to go there with Ren," I pant, continuing to clamber. "Ren promised to take him. It's remote. It's abandoned. Ren knows I'll know to look for them there, but no one else will."

It's a cold, dark night by the time we reach the world above. I run straight up Candlemaker Row, past the Gruff Pub and Avizandum to get to the main road. Past the now-unmoving statue of Greyfriars Bobby, the one that started it all.

"Now what?" I ask myself, breathing heavily. "Freddy?"

"Yes?"

"I may need you to use your powers."

He smarts slightly at my words but fixes me with a sincere expression. "What do you need?"

I look at the cars driving by us, heading toward the Royal Mile and then the city center. Then I spot a young man on a motorcycle. I grit my teeth and turn back to Freddy.

"I need you to get that man to give us his bike. Just to borrow."

Freddy acts quickly. As the man slows down his bike to wait in traffic, Freddy approaches.

"You need to lend us your vehicle and wait here

by Bobby's statue until we come back to return it," Freddy says calmly and composedly.

The man's expression goes from bemusement to surprise and then to complete serenity. He smiles and swings his leg off the bike, allowing Freddy to grab the handlebars.

"Of course," the man says happily. "I'll just wait here."

I don't hesitate. I leap onto the bike and grab the handles. Freddy gets on behind me.

"We need to get to Leith," I shout over the noise. "It's the quickest way to water. You navigate and I'll drive."

"You sure?" yells Freddy.

I've ridden a quad bike a few times, how different can it be?

"Let's go! Don't let my beret fall off!"

CHAPTER NINETEEN

RAMYA KNOX IS AWAY WITH THE KELPIES

It's good to learn new things about yourself. Right now, I'm learning that I am a reckless driver.

I dodge and dart and zoom down the mound toward Princes Street like a fiend. Freddy grips on tight from behind, swearing each time the bike becomes slightly airborne. It's exhilarating and addictive, but I don't have much energy to enjoy it. I'm focused on the island.

"This'll show that occupational therapist!" I yell as we skid around a corner and head out of town toward Leith. "She said I would probably never drive! Look at me now!"

"I feel queasy!" Freddy shouts back. "Take a left here!"

I move my body in tandem with the bike and we

zip through the dimly lit streets of Edinburgh toward Inchkeith with speed and unapologetic need.

When we finally reach the waterfront, Freddy helps me slow the bike and I dismount hurriedly.

It's suddenly very quiet. Deceptively calm.

"This is it," I say gently. I kneel down by the water and rest my palms on the cold surface.

"Ramya—"

"Thank you for your help, Freddy. Now I need you to take that bike back to its owner."

"Ramya, what if this is all a trap?"

Oh, Freddy. Of course it's a trap. But I still have to go. "I'll be fine. Leave."

He hesitates. I turn back to the water. I press my face down to its cold, unforgiving exterior and embrace the feeling of it against my skin.

"It's me," I say to the icy current. "I know what to do."

By the time I lift my head up, they are here. At least ten of them. All standing in the shallows of the vast river, illuminated by the moon. Their watery bodies and silver eyes glisten in the pale light.

"Whoa," Freddy murmurs, staring out at the herd in disbelief.

"I know what happened to your friend," I say sorrowfully, addressing the kelpie at the front of the herd. "It's awful. I'm so sorry."

They don't move. Not one hair.

"Freddy." I speak very softly. "They're not sure about you. Back up a bit."

I hear him moving, pulling the bike with him. "Ramya, are you sure—"

"I'm fine," I repeat firmly. "Go."

I feel him waiting, still reluctant to leave. Then he gets on the bike. I listen to him drive away, all the while watching the kelpies. When silence falls over the area once more, I step into the water. Letting it push against my calves.

"I couldn't find the witch for you," I say miserably. "But I have a plan. There's a siren on that island. A cruel one. He has a member of my family. If you help me . . . if you get me to that island and help me, I'll be able to keep him there."

A long pause. Then the first kelpie moves closer. I step farther into the river, breathing steadily and trying to forget the stories told of water horses that drowned people in rivers and ponds.

The giant creature continues to walk toward me, treading on water with ease. I step forward again.

His long face is soon before mine. Mere inches away. He snorts an exhale, a spray of water hitting my face. I close my eyes and don't move.

I wait for what feels like too long. Then feel a cold, wet face press against mine.

I don't know if my face is wet from the spray or

from tears, but I'm shaking with gratitude. I turn my face to one of his long, slender ears and I whisper my plan.

The kelpie brays and then turns to the others. The rest of the herd slips beneath the surface, and I watch as their dark shadows move in all directions, out into deeper water.

I look out. The island seems farther away from this part of the waterfront. Not as near as the view from the dock at Newhaven. It's the same river, though. The same island.

And I'm going to get there.

It starts to rain as the kelpie canters over to me. He stops in front of me, regarding me with his frightening eyes. Every inch of his gaze is a warning. Telling me not to make him regret this.

I bow my head.

The kelpie does the same. Bowing his head and lowering his body so that his large back is closer to the water. I move toward him with tentative steps, my heart beating so loudly, I know he must be able to hear it.

I place a hand on his mane. It's icy cold and slippery. I pause, unsure of how to proceed. There is no saddle, no stirrups or reins.

The kelpie tosses his head, as if to say, "Get on with it, human."

I grip the mane as gently as possible and hoist myself onto his wet, glassy back. The kelpie's tail swishes and he stamps one hoof against the river.

The message is clear: Hold on.

I lean forward and wrap both arms around the kelpie's broad neck. It's my own way of saying that I trust him. That despite all the stories of travelers being drowned by kelpies and dragged down to the stones at the bottom of the river, I trust him. I want to help him.

I'm not putting faith in other people's stories anymore. Only my own.

The kelpie takes off in a breath. I stifle a scream as he gallops at full speed, faster than I could have conjured up in a dream. His hooves hit the water with the power of a blacksmith forging metal, and I have to grip tightly to avoid being flung off into the depths.

The kelpie runs in a pulsing, powerful rhythm. The water becomes rougher as we venture farther into the heart of the river, and I gasp each time we leap over a wave and land. I expect us to sink deep beneath the black surface of the water, but the kelpie maintains balance upon the river as if we're hurtling through a forest.

Inchkeith comes into view through the mist and fog of a dark October night in Edinburgh.

I'm ready.

As we near the patch of land, the kelpie rears up and makes one last leap. He flies onto the banks of the island and comes to a halt. I push all the air out of my lungs and close my eyes for a second. I dismount unsteadily and turn to face the creature with damp eyes and a trembling hand.

"Thank you."

The kelpie snorts and tosses his mane.

"Remember the plan?" I murmur as I glance at my surroundings. It's a small island from a distance, but now that I stand on it, it seems larger. I cannot see Marley or Ren, just dirt and green and stone ruins. It's not completely flat.

Then, a few feet away, I spot it.

It's so dim on Inchkeith, without any unnatural light, but I can make out the remains of Ren's boat. I recognize it from the dock at Newhaven. It's hit something, a rock perhaps, and is full of water.

The kelpie sinks beneath the river as I stagger over to the boat. I'm suddenly so afraid of what might be there.

No one. The boat is empty.

I heave a sigh of relief. They reached the island, they're here. There's no way to leave now that their boat is clearly buckled.

I walk erratically, heading farther into Inchkeith. It's so silent, all I can hear is the singing of the water. The lights from the famous Forth bridges gleam in the distance. I know the people in the cars and the trains won't see me. They probably cannot even see the island. Edinburgh feels far away. I take one last look at the city in the distance as I head uphill, nearing the core of the island.

I come down a small mound to an open square with rubble and ruins dotted all around. Then I see him. Sitting with his back to me, one hundred yards away. I feel a surge of adrenaline inside as I yell, "Marley!"

His head whips around, and I can see that his face is streaked with dirt and tears. I sprint down the mound and start running toward him.

"Ramya, run!"

"Marley, get to the water!" I scream as I point to the shore in the distance. "Get to the water now!"

Marley struggles to his feet and limps toward the water, and I take off after him.

Only to feel something crash into me from the left, knocking me to the ground. I swear as my cheek grazes harshly against the tiny stones. Marley freezes and looks back in anguish.

"Get to the *water*!" I bellow, wriggling and fighting as Ren's boot presses down hard between my shoulder blades.

"Let her go!"

I shake my head frantically as Marley starts running back toward us.

I need him to get to the water. I need him to be *safe*. I need him to get out of here and never turn around.

"Stop." Ren's voice is relaxed and amused.

Marley slows to a halt, but his face shows how much he is fighting the compulsion. Ren releases his weight from my back, and I scramble to my feet, darting away so I can face him head-on.

"You are a strange one," Ren says to me. His lower half is wet, probably a result of the boat almost sinking. His sleeves are rolled up and his eyes are shrewd and questioning, looking at me intently. "I never counted on you."

He seems so relaxed. His face almost pleasant.

"You're a siren," I spit, glaring at him. "I've known for a while. I should have smashed that paperweight over your head on the night your little fae robbery went sideways."

"So aggressive, Ramya," he laughs.

"I see through you," I snarl. "Your compulsions don't work on me."

"Oh, I'm well aware," he tells me. "When I told the fae to dispatch the two of you, I didn't realize . . . but no matter. Lucky for you, your aunt Leanna was there. I was hoping to kill the two of you and your nobody of an aunt and frame it as a tragic accident."

"Why keep Aunt Leanna alive?"

"She's important to too many people. No one would care about Opal. I knew that without ever meeting her. Could tell at your grandfather's funeral. But Leanna, no. She has too many guardians. Alas, a foiled plan. But here you are now."

I wipe some gravel from my face and glare at him. If I can distract him long enough, Marley can get to the water. I look to my cousin, silently trying to communicate all of this in my face. He nods subtly and starts taking minimal, tiny steps backward toward the shore.

"I knew my targets had a daughter," Ren muses calmly. "But all I was told was she was an emotionally stunted little head case. Poor academic performer, barely able to hold a pen. I certainly never thought I had to worry about you."

Edging. Ever so slowly and slightly to the water.

"Why are they your targets?"

"Portia has such wonderful vision. She really sees the bigger picture. She wanted me here before she arrives. Did you know most people believe whatever they hear on television? It's an absolute dream for a siren. Portia has such wonderful ideas."

My stomach flips over at this piece of information. "To do what?"

He smiles but it's a horrible thing. "You'll never find out, I'm afraid. Need-to-know basis for now."

"You underestimate this city," I tell him quietly. My eyes flit to the river. "You underestimated me."

"Oh, Ramya," he laughs. "Perhaps. But you're not getting off this island."

I feign shock. I pretend to be disturbed by his words. "What?"

"You think I care what happens to that nit?" Ren asks, jerking a thumb at Marley, whose face crumples at the words. "That's why you came here, isn't it? You thought you could both be home in time for breakfast and the sun coming up? Not a chance. I knew you would come; I was hoping for it. He's the bait and you're the tiny fish."

I suddenly notice a knife tucked into his belt. It's a vain, narcissistic thing. Narrow and sharp, with patterns engraved on it. But it would still do a lot of damage.

"Why lure me out to an island?" I ask, humoring him. "You want the book?"

He smirks. "There's nothing in your book I don't already know. Sirens see through Glamour, too, Ramya. Just like you."

"If you start talking about how we're alike," I snarl, "I'll vomit."

"Now, I will admit," Ren says, touching one finger to the top of his blade and walking casually down toward the shore, causing me to mirror his movement while Marley backs up. "Some people are harder to influence than others. You get boringly principled people who don't budge, no matter how much power you put in your voice. But children are easy. Too easy. So when you wouldn't play ball, I knew something was different about you. Something your aunt Leanna had neglected to mention."

Marley has finally reached the shoreline. I stop, feeling relief but making sure not to show it.

"You really thought you could manipulate my parents to get your views on television?" I ask disdainfully.

He shrugs. "For a time. Your parents aren't like you; they're very susceptible. Most people are. Plus, television is quick. A lot of reach with not a lot of effort. But no. Sorry, Ramya, my biggest concern is having someone like you running around Edinburgh getting Hidden Folk overexcited."

"Overexcited?"

"I don't like an uprising. I don't like to see the natural order of things disturbed. You started putting ideas in their heads. Ideas about equality, about community. It's disgusting."

"It is not."

"It is!" he roars, causing Marley to whimper and me to jump back. His mask fully gone for a moment. "It's been centuries since we lived in the ocean. Did you work that one out? Drowning sailors isn't the cool thing anymore. It all became far too tricky when the ships got large. So we came to land. The land is our ocean now and our song is anywhere we want it to be."

"Do you know what I find so repulsive about you?" I say, my voice hard but quiet. "You and Portia, people like you, you do evil things. You rip families apart, you lie, and you manipulate and you hurt. But you try to make it seem so reasonable. You wrap evil ideas and deeds up in charm and make it seem practical and realistic. That's what's detestable. You pretend on top of everything else. You can't even own what you are."

I look to Marley. It's almost time. I feel the call of the salt and the cold and the spray, the energy of the river. In that strange way I have always done. The link between us, me and the water, something I've never been able to explain. I feel it strengthen.

I stare at my cousin and smile. He and my family have always been in a boat together. When the water is rocky, they stay in their vessel and take on the waves together. Rising and falling with each crash against the hull, never separating.

I have never been in that boat with the rest of them. I'm a strong swimmer. In the water, alone. Right now, I feel I'm watching that boat sail farther and farther away. Each bob of the water makes them a smaller speck in the distance.

We'll never be in that boat all together. But at least they'll be safe.

"It's all right, Marley," I say soothingly. One tear slipping free. "It's going to be all right."

He stares back in confusion, but I return my attention to Ren.

"There's one thing you don't understand. I knew you wanted me to come here. As soon as I worked out you were taking Marley here, I knew what had to happen. After what you tried to do that night in the shop, I knew it was all a trap. I'm a threat to you. Not him, not anyone else. There's no witch after all. No one will come and save me. My family will be out searching for Marley. Whatever trance you put over Aunt Leanna, it will end. She would've searched every corner of the world. My grandmother, too."

I feel the catch in my voice, but I go on.

"But no one is looking for me, Ren. Not me. But Marley? He's special. He's beloved. He's the best apple on the tree."

I take a deep breath, feeling the shift in the water. The oncoming movement.

"I'm the black sheep. The one the flock doesn't mind cutting loose. No one's going to come searching for me. The one person who thought I was anything special is gone," I say, remembering my grandpa's face. I touch my beret. The very same one he gave me all those years ago, before my first-ever experience with a magical creature.

"There's something more powerful than your voice and your lies, something you will never understand," I conclude softly.

"Is it love?" snorts Ren, thoroughly entertained by me. "Family? Please, Ramya, I always thought you were at least a realist. Don't get soppy on me, please."

He laughs a laugh as cold as the water. Which is about to break.

"What don't I understand, then?" he jeers. "Enlighten me."

I turn to stare at the water. He follows my gaze, his smile slipping a touch. In a fluid flash of movement, the kelpie rears out of the river, half human, half water horse. He grabs Marley around the waist and hurls him onto his back. Marley's face is a picture of shock and astonishment as the kelpie turns and starts galloping back to Edinburgh. To land, to safety.

Ren roars in fury and starts toward the spot that the kelpie appeared from, but he is already a shadow on the surface of the water. Far away and safe from Ren's rage over his foiled plans.

"Sacrifice," I say brokenly. "You don't understand sacrifice."

He stares at me, as if seeing me for the first time. Then his face morphs into cold satisfaction once more.

"No matter," he says evenly. "I never needed him. It was always you."

"Do it," I reply. "I'm sorry you had to go to such dramatic lengths to get what you want."

I don't tell him my secret. That another siren knows where I am. Ren will kill me, yes. I knew coming here to save Marley meant that. But Freddy is my hidden ace. He will make sure Ren doesn't get away with it. I can keep him on this island, surrounded by kelpies who won't let him cross the water, until Freddy knows I'm not coming back. Then the authorities will come for him.

"Ah, Ramya," Ren says. "I'm really doing you a favor. The world was never made for someone like you. I know all the adults in your life probably tell you that it will all get easier. But it won't. You can try to follow all their rules, but they will never accept you. You will never be enough because being enough is decided by them. And you're not one of them."

His words are strange. There is something resigned hiding inside them. "I'm not like you," I say.

"But you are," he says plainly. "I know how it feels. You've tried everything, haven't you? You have been and done everything they want. Or say they want. And for what? To be standing here alone. No one here to fight for you. You're ready to die for a family that's only ever tried to change you."

"Not him," I say, and it feels peaceful to say. "Not my grandpa. He never tried to change me. Never wanted me to. I'm sorry you don't know what that feels like. To have someone believe in you, and not because they're under some kind of evil spell. Because, even though he's gone, I still feel him here. That's the best kind of magic."

"I'll say one thing for you." Ren speaks confidently, standing opposite me with enough space between us for it to look like we're about to duel. "I didn't expect this. Under all that sarcasm, all that hostility and the acting up. I didn't think you actually had it in you."

"You should have."

I'm like water. I may seem calm, or I may appear aggressive. You can't tell until you're actually there. I was never an island after all. I was always the water. Changing and coursing and pulsing with life.

If I have to be the water to push my family to safety, to get them to that lighthouse and out of the storm, I'll do it. Even if it means I sink.

"This was certainly more interesting than I expected," Ren tells me genially. "But there's more power in you. It's not just that you can see through Glamour. I expect even you realize that."

I stare at him, saying nothing.

"I spoke to that faerie," he adds coolly. "You filled that room with water, didn't you?"

I don't react. I suppose I knew deep down. That it was me. The leak in the house, the shattered glasses at school. I suppose a part of me always knew.

"I can't have you growing more powerful," Ren says in that same reasonable tone. "Then they really will follow you, Ramya. They might follow you anywhere. And I can't have that."

I watch his next movements as if they are happening very slowly. He reaches for his knife and raises it high over his head, preparing to throw. I watch his hand release it.

The blade soars toward me with the accuracy of a missile.

I close my eyes.

CHAPTER TWENTY

THE HEARTBROKEN WITCH

I hear a gasping sound and the soft clang of metal. My eyes are still closed. I feel wind suddenly gather all around me, causing flecks of dirt and sand to brush against me.

But no impact from the knife. If it's struck me, I don't feel any pain.

I open my eyes.

I see Ren, still where he stood, but now wearing an expression of panic and astonishment. The knife is frozen in midair. Exactly between the two of us, suspended in the breeze and completely motionless. I can't understand it.

Suddenly, it fractures. It cracks and breaks and then destroys itself, becoming a thousand tiny particles. I watch as they hover, suspended in the air, then soar as one into the sky and over the island. The tiny droplets of what was once Ren's knife scatter about like dust. A dangerous weapon broken apart and turned into particles of metal rain.

Ren's eyes are fixed over my head, full of alarm and amazement. And the first real glimmer of fear.

I turn. And there she is.

Levitating a foot above the ground, one arm out-stretched, is Opal. Her face is as calm and as cool as I've ever seen it. There is even a glint in her eye. She stares back at Ren with great intensity.

"Get away from her," she tells him, her words slow but completely laced in menace. "Or I'll break you."

Ren snarls and charges her. She raises her arm higher and then snaps it down, like cracking a whip. I watch, stunned, as a bolt of electricity shoots from her hand and hits Ren in the face. He curses and falls back, clutching his cheek and glaring at her.

"It was you," I say, amazed. "All along, it was you."

She glances at me and smiles. It's the most trans-formative expression, turning her into a person I've never met.

"Watch my high C, Ramya."

I let out a scream of joyous laughter, the kind you can only feel when you're happy to be alive, and I delight in watching her raise both of her palms. She pushes them and a wave of energy flies across the stony beach toward the siren. He falls flat on his back while green grass morphs into rope, snaking around him until he is completely bound.

It was her all along. The one we all disregarded. The one they pretended was weak.

The one who is like me.

As Ren twists and wriggles, fighting his bindings, Opal moves with casual grace and calm. I scramble over and she puts one arm around my shoulders, squeezing me tightly.

"So listen," she says to Ren, leaning over him and grinning. "I've disliked a lot of my sister's boyfriends throughout the years, but you have to be the slimiest one yet."

Ren looks as if he's trying to spit.

"Release me!" he barks, and I can tell he is putting all his influence into his voice. "Set me free. You want to let me go, witch. You want me to be released."

"No, I don't think I do," Opal says breezily. "Have you not worked it out, Lavrentiy?"

She pulls me close to her and squeezes me again, and I squeeze back. I press my face into her side and cling on.

"We're the same," she says cheerfully. "I see through Glamour, just like this one. Your vocal tricks won't work on either of us, I'm afraid."

Ren lets out a strangled scream of frustration, his eyes burning with hatred.

"What should we do with him?" Opal asks me conspiratorially.

"Hand him over to the police?"

"I'll talk my way out," hisses Ren. "You just watch me."

"Good point," Opal says. "Then I guess you stay here. These bindings will rot away eventually. After that, the kelpies can have you."

She turns and walks away from his writhing form, gently moving me with her. She kneels in front of me once we're a safe distance away, and she starts inspecting me for injuries.

"I'm fine," I say reassuringly. My chattering teeth and shaking hands give me away.

"No, you're not," she says, not unkindly. "You've been let down by about every adult in your life and then been through a traumatic event."

"I didn't think anyone would come for me," I say, more to myself than to her.

She looks up at me. Her face—it's so unlike Mum's and Aunt Leanna's.

Eyes like Grandpa's.

"Ramya," she says, and her voice breaks. "I'm so, so sorry. We've all let you down."

"It's okay," I reply. "You're here now."

"You came to save Marley. Why didn't you wait?

We could have helped. We could have come with you."

"There wasn't time to wait," I say truthfully. "I waited all those years for Mum and Grandpa to make up, and it never happened. I don't wait anymore."

"Your grandfather," Ren yells suddenly, wriggling in his bindings, "was a meddling goat. Just like you, brat. Portia remembers you, Ramya. She remembers your grandfather. You'll meet your end soon, same as he did, witch."

Something settles in Opal's eyes. Something finalizes. She gets to her feet and turns to face Ren. His eyes search greedily for signs of hurt, desperate to see the impact of his cruel words.

Opal holds both hands out in front of her and power blasts toward the siren. It's so strong, she has to dig her heels into the ground, as if she is fighting against the wind. I watch in amazement as Ren's body begins to transform. When he realizes what is happening, he starts to curse Opal, but her face is blank, immune to his fury.

When she finally releases all the power she was harnessing, she collapses to the ground. I move next to her, checking that she is all right. Then I look over at where Ren was lying.

Now he is a statue. An unmoving, unemotional statue of stone.

"Whoa," I breathe.

Opal groans slightly and I rush back over. She lies down on her back and places her hands on her stomach, focusing on her breath and staring up at the stars.

"That's about all I have in me tonight, I think," she says dryly.

"You turned him to stone," I murmur, looking back over at the statue.

"Well," she says. "He was irritating me."

I laugh. A nearly hysterical sound. It causes her eyes to open. She watches me carefully.

"Everything," I say, glancing around at the vast sky. The pinpricks of bright light shining down on us. The pale moon lighting up the dark water. The dramatic bridges, the firefly lights of the city. "Everything is going to be different now, isn't it?"

She smiles a weak smile. "Yes."

I exhale. "I know I should have asked for help. But I'm not very good at that."

There's a beat of silence before she says, "I'm the same."

"You are?"

"When you're wired a little differently," she says quietly, "you learn pretty quickly to rely on yourself. You can only be told 'That's a stupid question' so many times. So you stop asking. You go it alone."

I close my eyes and nod. "That's exactly it."

"Kid. I've been exactly where you are." She taps my beret. "I just wasn't as stylish."

"You're the Heartbroken Witch, Aunt Opal."

She winces. "Well, I didn't choose that name."

"Heartbroken about Grandpa?"

She waves her hand wearily and something floats out of her coat pocket. It floats into the air and unfolds in front of me.

It's a handkerchief. The one Grandpa showed me all those years ago.

"This was his," I say tearfully. "He showed it to me once."

I squeeze it. Remembering the last time I saw it. The last time I held it.

"Yes."

"You must really miss him, Aunt Opal."

I always thought heartbreak meant screaming in anguish. I thought it meant tears and shouting and wailing. I thought it was this loud and overt explosion that made everyone look at you.

Aunt Opal didn't have a heart of ice after all. Instead, one of glass. One that was fragile and quiet. Just trying to stay in one piece.

Her eyes are like the water. Shining and dark. "He was the one I could talk about magic with no matter what. So after he was gone . . . I didn't feel like doing it anymore."

"But you can do so much!" I say in wonder.

She looks at me, slightly amused. "And you will too."

"What?"

"Ramya, I didn't fill that room in the underground market with water. You did."

I stare down at my open palms. "I suppose I did."

"That's why they've been trying to . . ."

"Get rid of me?"

She nods, seeming torn. "I don't think hiding you is an option anymore. Not today, and maybe not tomorrow, but soon it might be a good idea to start teaching you how to really control what you can do."

"You could do that?"

"Yes. All your power is currently tied to strong emotion. I can help you master it. So you can use it when you choose to."

I feel something settle inside my chest. "Thank you."

I look out at the vast river and spot something. I get to my feet and approach the water. It's the kelpie. The one who brought me here and who saved Marley.

"Where's my cousin—is he okay?" I call out to the shadowy creature.

He transforms into his partially human state. "With his mother."

I exhale in relief. I feel Opal get to her feet next to

me. She's weak and shaken, but she stands tall and faces the kelpie.

"I'm sorry for what happened to Cella."

I watch silently. Cella must have been the young kelpie that the fae pulled from the shallows.

The kelpie regards Opal, without giving away a single thing. "Are you back, witch?"

Opal looks to me, and I smile. She does too. Then turns to the kelpie.

"Yes. I'm back."

While it seems impossible for a kelpie to show a smile, the echo of one forms on the creature's face. He bows his head sharply, then transforms into his natural shape, with the fluidity and flexibility of the water he stands in.

The kelpie trots across the river and bows again.

"How did you get to the island?" I ask Opal, suddenly realizing she probably did not ride a kelpie like I did.

Despite how burned out she looks, she shows me. She hovers half a foot off the ground.

I clap a hand over my mouth. "Oh my God. Can you teach me to do that?"

She laughs tiredly. "Maybe. It's very difficult. It exhausts you pretty quickly."

"Still!"

The dreams I have had about flying. How many times I have sat in a therapist's office, or a meeting with the school counselor, wishing the window would open and I could soar out and away.

To know there's the slightest possibility . . . it's too exciting. Too overwhelming.

"How do you do it?" I ask breathlessly. "A broom?"

"No," she laughs, reaching a hand out to the kelpie. He places his nose against her palm. "I suppose it's a kind of telekinesis. It won't take you for miles, or up over the clouds, but it can get you to an island to save your reckless niece if need be."

I grin sheepishly. "That's amazing."

The kelpie snorts and lowers the front half of his body once more. I take the hint, mounting the watery shape-shifter like a horse. Opal watches unsurely from the island beach.

"It's all right," I say encouragingly. "He won't drag us under."

The kelpie tramps his foot impatiently. Opal gingerly mounts up behind me. I feel her legs tighten, gripping the kelpie's sides.

"Let's take the scenic route," I whisper to the kelpie. Then I speak over my shoulder. "Hold on!"

"Oh, God," mutters Aunt Opal, and then she lets out a startled yelp as the kelpie bolts like a horse running a great, watery racetrack. I release a cry of exhilaration and grip the kelpie around the neck.

We are indeed taking the scenic route. Instead of

heading for Edinburgh, the kelpie gallops toward the Forth Road Bridge. I scream in delight and close my eyes, feeling the spray of the cold water as the creature canters at great speed. At one point, the kelpie dives down under the river and back up again, in a split second. We both shout in surprise and I laugh, feeling completely free as the kelpie continues to bound along the river.

I've never ridden a real horse, and now I don't think I ever can. It can't feel like this. It cannot feel as heady, as amazing. Each leap, each smack of the kelpie's slippery hoof against the surface of the water makes my heart and lungs feel like they're exiting my body and falling back into place. Each beat of the gallop is a live wire up and down my spine.

The three huge bridges are up ahead. First a railway bridge, which we storm underneath with pulsing quickness. Then the second bridge looms. It's a suspension bridge, about five hundred feet high.

"No time like the present!" Opal suddenly calls.

Before I can ask what she means, she grips me around the waist. Abruptly, we are airborne. We soar up and toward the bridge while the kelpie continues to gallop, now without any riders. He soon becomes merged with the river once more, gone from view.

"This is amazing!" I shriek, half delighted and half afraid as we fly toward the top point of the enormous bridge. I grip onto her arms, too scared to

fully accept that she is doing this. We have no para-
chute, no wires. We are in midair because of magic.

Opal carries us both up to stand atop the suspension bridge. I grab onto her as the wind beats against
us. Vehicles are small down below us, like toy cars.

"That was incredible!" I shout over the wind.

"It was!" she shouts back. "Now it's your turn."

My face falls. "What?"

She grips my hand tightly and we both look down
at the five-hundred-foot drop to the wide, flowing
river below.

"It's not a spell, Ramya," she yells over the noise.
"It's not dust or tricks or even happy thoughts. It's
your brain. That brilliant brain that's made different."

As the wind lashes all around me, causing me to
grip my beret, I can feel the years of "You can't."
All the confusing, pathological conversations that
stripped away a ball gown of self-esteem until it became rags.

Yes, there are things I probably will have difficulty doing for the rest of my life. Things that might
come naturally to other people. Why did they never
help to find all the unbelievable things I *can* do?

"Don't ever try this without me!" Opal says
firmly. I nod.

Gripping Opal's hand, I fall forward. Down
toward the water. I yell, a primal sound. As the air

changes all around me, I feel something hook inside my stomach. I feel it connect with the electric part of my brain they told me wasn't made right.

It now feels utterly right. I can do anything.

I lean into the connection and suddenly, I'm no longer falling. I'm no longer the faller.

I fly. Ahead toward the horizon, Opal beside me. I skim over the water of the immense Firth of Forth, letting my fingers brush the river. I'm propelled onward with a new sense of freedom.

I cry in astonishment as we suddenly find ourselves surrounded by kelpies. They leap and dive underneath us, alongside us. When I lose concentration for a split second, the water seems to rise beneath me. It presses into my body, assisting me. Helping me.

The stimulation I'm feeling is the magic. It's what is letting me do this. The very thing I always shied away from.

I'm flying.

CHAPTER TWENTY-ONE

COMMUNITY

Opal and I arrive at the Grassmarket. The secret one, underground. Apparently, there are lots of tunnels that connect certain shops with the hidden area underneath. One tunnel is in Leanna's shop. The market is full of familiar faces, who smile at me in a knowing way as Opal and I enter the underground square. I see Murrey in one group, Erica in another.

We find my other aunt and Marley, shaken but safe in one of the alcoves of the market.

They both leap to their feet when they see us, but my happiness at the sight of them is short-lived.

My parents are there too, taking in the market with barely concealed terror. When Mum sees me, I brace myself for anger. Instead, she starts to cry. Dad as well.

It's like when I fell from the chairlift. The worry overtook anything else in them.

All of us sit around the table, too exhausted to speak. Me, my cousin, my dad, Mum, and her two sisters.

"Well," Mum says at last, her voice hoarse and tired. "I think we all have a lot to discuss."

"Just maybe not tonight," Leanna murmurs, resting her cheek on the top of Marley's head.

My cousin keeps trying to catch my eye, but I'm tired. I lean my head back on the wall of the booth and close my eyes.

"I'm confused," Dad says, and his voice is a garbled croak of complete bewilderment. "Cass, I really don't—"

"Not tonight," Mum says swiftly. "The children are exhausted."

I hate when adults blame their own problems on us. Marley and I are tired, but no more than they are. Aunt Leanna is paler than a ghost. Mum looks the same way she does when she comes home from an eighteen-hour flight.

Only Opal is steady.

"YOU!"

I don't need to turn my head to know who it is. The venom is enough for me to recognize it's one of the fae.

When I do get to my feet and face them, I see

it's the one who came hunting for me in the Gruff Pub. The one who almost broke some poor person's fingers. I notice he's wearing something on a chain around his neck.

It's an ear. What looks like a horse's ear.

A kelpie's ear. Cella's ear.

I glare at him, righteous anger humming inside me. There is no cruel amusement in his gaze this time. Just cold fury.

"Surprised to see me?" I ask icily.

"How did you get off that island?" he snarls. "And where is—"

"Lavrentiy won't be around these parts anymore," I tell him calmly. "But you're free to go and visit him on Inchkeith. I expect he'll be there for a long time. Like, maybe forever. He's part of the scenery now. Gathering moss."

Understanding creeps into the faerie's face. It strikes me that Ren perhaps promised the fae something in return for their cooperation. Whatever that was, they won't be getting it now.

"I'd stick to the mainland, if I were you," I add, staring pointedly at the ear around his neck. "The kelpies don't forget."

Fear flickers in his bright, white eyes, but it's quickly replaced with rage. He advances toward me.

And something incredible happens.

Murrey steps forward, his fangs bared in a hiss.

The sweet-tempered vampire who confided in me is temporarily gone, now staring down the faerie like a predator.

Erica, and a number of other trolls, come forward as well. They stand in front of me like a dam in a river, blocking the faerie's access to me, causing him to stagger back a few steps.

"What are you doing?" spits the faerie, glaring at his fellow Hidden Folk in startled confusion. "This doesn't concern you."

Three sprites, all brightly colored, float dreamily down from the ceiling beams. They land on the shoulders of those in front of me.

Marley stands up next to me on my right. Freddy appears, taking the spot on my left.

"You're here?" I whisper.

He smiles. "Dropped off the bike. Good to see you made it out."

I flush and turn back to staring at the faerie. He has spotted Freddy.

"Your mother would be ashamed," he says callously.

I frown. I don't know what the faerie means by that, but Freddy stares back in blatant defiance.

"I think all of us," he says quietly, "are getting really sick of your influence."

I step forward, galvanized by the group that has formed all around me.

"You're going to stop terrorizing this town."

The faerie makes a high, screeching sound that hurts my ears. "Or what?" he snarls.

Suddenly, Aunt Opal and Mum are among the group. Opal smiles sweetly and opens her palm, revealing a crackling bolt of charge, ready to be fired. The faerie stumbles backward at the sight of it, knocking a stall over.

"This girl is protected," Opal says smoothly. "And I'm done with my time off."

She steps forward, bends down, and snatches the kelpie's ear free from the faerie's neck. Hidden Folk throughout the market gasp and murmur among themselves at the sight of the Heartbroken Witch returned.

"You will never have so much free rein to be cruel again," she says softly to the faerie.

Something has caught my eye.

Mum's palm is also open, exactly like Aunt Opal's. In it are small, flickering but very ferocious flames.

My jaw drops. I slap Marley on the arm, and he stares at both of his aunts as if they're every bit as magical as the Hidden Folk we're being protected by.

Which, I suppose, they are.

"No way," he mutters, staring at the fire.

The faerie pushes out of the wreckage he's made

and takes off toward a tunnel, disappearing from sight. A slow-building cheer starts to fill the room.

"Community," I say softly, gazing around at the army of Hidden Folk that stepped forward. "You were right, Freddy."

It's what we have, and they do not.

I catch Mum's eye and nod at the fading flames in her palm.

"Yes," I say emphatically. "We do have a lot to discuss."

★

A WHILE LATER, Mum tells me I have to sleep before she will even consider telling me about what I saw. Judging by the slightly green tinge on Dad's face as we drive home in the car, it was all a surprise to him as well. He is also grappling with the underground Grassmarket and all the unglamoured creatures.

"Did I see little fae?" he asks dazedly.

"Sprites," I correct him before yawning and closing my eyes.

CHAPTER TWENTY-TWO

O COUSIN

I woke up about thirteen hours later, in my own bed, having gone to sleep with the feeling of flying.

All Mum would say as we had breakfast was that if I wanted to stay home from school, that was all right. This was quite revolutionary, as Mum is usually the kind of person to say that unless your leg is hanging off, you're fine. I decided I wanted to go to school. Boring, humdrum normality might be the antidote after a strange night full of magic.

Mum said we would talk when I got home.

It's lunchtime. I'm now sitting at the large water fountain that doesn't work, going over history notes.

"Rasputin," I say to Marley, who has appeared in front of me. "Now, there was a siren."

He laughs weakly and then hovers. I don't look at him.

"Ramya, I'm so sorry."

"It's fine," I say, putting my history book into my bag. "You were under a kind of spell."

"He spent the whole day before you came to see me telling Mum and me how bad for us you were," he says miserably. "But I should have fought him harder."

"So Aunt Leanna wasn't doing her accounts?" I question. "He wasn't letting her answer the phone."

"Yes."

I puff out a breath. "Marley, he's not coming back."

"I know," Marley says. "Mum and I started seeing through it before he took me to Inchkeith. I tried to fight it."

"I know," I say. "It's not your fault."

"I still said those awful things. They aren't true."

"Marley." I speak steadily. "Magic is this weird, eccentric thing that isn't predictable or consistent. Your mum can make plants bloom. Mine can apparently influence fire. Aunt Opal can fly, for goodness' sake! And Ren? He can manipulate. That was his power. He was really good at it. So good at it, I didn't feel any of the initial worries I felt when I met Portia. He was so adept."

I remember the way Ren spoke about how we

were alike. But we're not. He chose the easy road. He chose to be a monster. Because a monster always chooses. That's what makes them evil. I know because I've had the same choice. I've been rejected and poked and prodded enough times for me to choose. When you're never allowed to be the hero, becoming their villain seems inevitable.

I finally glance up at Marley. "I'm starting to realize that if you've met one magical creature, that's it. You've met one magical creature. They're all so different. But Ren . . . he was bad. He didn't care about anyone but himself. He wanted us either fighting or not speaking at all. Because that's how you make people easy to control. You isolate them. You get them lonely. You make them afraid."

Marley's whole face is an apology. "I was afraid. I still can't believe you came to the island."

I look at him frankly. "I would do it again."

I don't want to explain everything that happened on that island right now. Some parts might be private forever. Marley cared about Ren; he doesn't need the specific details of his demise.

"Ren said I would end up like Grandpa," I reveal. I don't want to fully admit how frightening I found his words. His use of Portia's name, his vindictive smirk.

"You're a lot like Grandpa."

I squint at him, surprised. "What?"

"You remind me of him. You have the same personality."

Marley hardly talks about Grandpa. Marley hardly talks about anything unless it's found inside a textbook. He reacts to things that other people say. He lets me order him around.

"I miss him lots," he goes on quietly. "We used to eat sandwiches in Greyfriars together when he came down from Loch Ness."

I swallow. "You were in Greyfriars when I found you that night."

"I thought . . ." He kicks an invisible stone with the toe of his shoe. "I thought if witches and magic are real, maybe ghosts are too."

I blink three times in quick succession. "Okay."

"You are. You really are like him, Ramya."

I didn't know people could inherit character traits like they do a nose or a pair of eyes.

"I don't feel like I have the right to be sad."

I tell Marley this, even though I'm afraid to say it. It's something I've been trying to put into words since I first heard the news. Since the moment I looked into the receptionist's eyes and heard her say the words.

"Why?"

I shrug. "I didn't know him. I met him a couple of times. I never saw or spoke to him again after that night with Portia. Why should I get to feel sad and mopey about someone I've met a handful of times? I didn't know him like you did."

Marley says nothing for a while. I imagine I've scared him away from this topic of conversation when—

"He saw you all the time when you were a baby."

I can feel my face frowning. "He did?"

"Yeah. The house in Loch Ness is full of photographs. You and Grandpa at the hospital when you were born. Him pushing you in a stroller. Him sitting next to you when you were still too young to crawl. It's all there. On the wall."

I feel a familiar ache. It twinges at his words. "I don't remember."

"Of course you don't. But he did. It happened. Somewhere, in your brain, you do remember. Some part of you knows. That's probably the part that wants to be sad. You don't have to earn being sad. You're allowed to be. That part of you probably needs to be."

I stare at him. "You're the smartest person I know, Marley."

I know it's the compliment he most wants to hear, but it also happens to be true.

"I'm so sorry."

"I know you are. But you were under a spell."

I don't want to press. I don't want to see if the magic merely brought out some hidden truths. The only thing that really mattered was the fact that Marley never would have said what he said, had he not been enchanted.

"I'm going to need you to make it up to me by helping, though."

Marley blinks at me quizzically, and with a touch of hope. "Helping you?"

"There's going to be more of them. Plus, Portia is still out there. Getting more and more powerful. It's going to take a lot to stop them. I'll need your brains."

Marley loves superhero films. He obsesses over them. But there is no superhero coming to fix this. It has to be us. We can't be the people on the street staring up at the battles in the sky, we have to make the change here on the ground.

Marley looks vulnerable for a moment. Slightly afraid. "What if . . . what if it happens again?"

I bump his shoulder lightly with my knuckles. "I won't let it."

He chews his lip but nods sagely.

"Or I could wear earmuffs?"

He smiles. I do too. Then he sits down next to me on the old fountain and starts telling me about how the baroness has been snooping in on his Gifted and Talented sessions.

"Did you two have a good half-term, then?"

We glance up and I find myself grinning as I see it

is Mr. Ishmael. He is slightly more rested than usual, but I would still bet he's been here since the very early hours before the first bell.

"It was eventful," I say, sharing a broad smirk with Marley. "Found a hidden underworld, met some evil fae. And now I'm a trainee witch."

Marley splutters but Mr. Ishmael just smiles indulgently.

"Certainly sounds like it was a lot of fun," he says, his tone very generous.

"It was," I cackle. Then I dig into a side pocket of my bag. "Here, Mr. Ishmael, I got you something."

I hand him some stiff terra-cotta-colored straw.

"Oh," he says, surprised. "Um. Thank you, Ramya."

"Wear it inside your jacket pocket for good luck," I say.

He gives me an appraising glance but nods as he does exactly that, tucking the Grassmarket purchase inside his jacket. I breathe a tiny sigh of relief.

"Ah, there you are, Mr. Ishmael."

I watch my Head of Year's face fall as he looks at someone behind us. I know, of course, who it is. I turn to see the baroness, standing in her ugly, badly tailored gray suit. Only this time, there is an additional accessory that makes my blood fizz with fury.

The beret she confiscated from me sits upon her terrible haircut.

"That's mine," I snap, glaring at her.

"Now, Ramya, hats are not permitted for students to wear, you know that."

She eyes me coolly, then returns her attention to Mr. Ishmael.

"I want to discuss the staff room," she says stridently. "I think it's a bad environment for your newly qualified teaching staff. They're far too social in there."

"Well," Mr. Ishmael says. His words are reasonable but his tone and expression firm. "I disagree. This is a very good school because our teachers put themselves through the wringer for our students. They need moments of respite, Baroness."

"Well," the baroness says in response, her eyes landing on me for a moment. "About that. I think some students would perhaps be better off in a less competitive environment. Ramya here is a fine example. Additional needs and struggling a little, I think."

A while ago, I would have got riled up. I would have exploded. I would have done myself a mischief. Now, as I stare up at the baroness wearing my beret, I feel flickers of excitement.

She wants to do this? We can do this.

"Additional needs?" I say artfully. "I'm dyspraxic and fantastic. I don't have any special needs, no one does. It's a label they stick on those of us who don't fit into the world's smallest uniform. I'm only on the unfortunate side of the numbers, lady. Listen, if there were more of me, I would maybe chuck a pathological mess of judgment on you."

A crowd of other students has started to gather all around the courtyard. I can see Patrick and Douglas with Mrs. Burns at the back.

"Take your fashion, for example," I say, projecting my voice so it's loud and carrying well. "Now, I am worried about you, Baroness. Anyone who would leave the house thinking this is an acceptable way to dress must suffer from some kind of delusion."

Sniggers start to rumble around the courtyard.

"Ramya," Mr. Ishmael says sternly, but I can hear the barely contained surprise and amusement in his teacherly voice. "That's enough."

"What do you think, Dr. Stewart-Napier?" I ask Marley in a mocking voice. "What is the prognosis for this unfortunate patient?"

"Well, Dr. Knox," Marley answers, catching on to the game immediately, "it's grim indeed, I fear."

"Mm, very grim indeed," I say, examining an imaginary clipboard that Marley has handed me. "Bad fashion, bullying nature, and tyrannical tendencies. I think a bout of electroshock therapy will do it!"

"Stop. Speaking," snarls the baroness, keeping

her voice low. "Or things will get very difficult for you."

"Oh, you don't get it?" I murmur, lurching forward on the large fountain. I speak softly now, so only she can hear me. "I know exactly what you are."

Does she think I'm stupid? Does she think I didn't notice how everyone begrudgingly obeyed her orders and demands, no matter how unreasonable they were? Does she think her muscling and manipulating inside the walls of this school have not been noted?

I know what she is.

"I know exactly what you are," I repeat. "And I've fought better. The last one was turned to stone. Your tricks don't work on people like me, Baroness. See, it's one of my additional needs. The need to stop people like you from inflicting harm. I take it real seriously. More seriously than handwriting workshops. More seriously than geometry. More seriously than even my academic career."

Her face becomes a picture of lividity in an instant. Rage contorts her face.

"Take a good look at this, educators," she says to the crowd all around us. "This is what a lack of discipline—"

"Bored of this!" I call, and I slap my hand against the old water fountain.

The fountain has been dry for decades, but I push all my newfound esteem and purpose into the touch. A crack forms on the other side and something miraculous happens.

Water, in a cold rush of defiance after years and years of slumber, shoots from the fountain. Soaking the baroness from top to bottom, the force of the water even causes her to stumble backward and land unceremoniously on the courtyard floor.

As people scream in delight and shock at the scene, some moving to bask in the spray of the water, I wave my hand subtly. The red beret soars from the head of the baroness and lands neatly in my palm. I place it triumphantly on my head, like the true heir wearing the crown a usurper tried to steal.

"Hey, Baroness," Marley calls. "It's not a hat. It's a beret."

"Good job," I mutter to him as we bump fists.

"She's one of them?" he says without moving his lips.

"Oh, yeah."

Mr. Ishmael hurries to help the baroness to her feet, but once she's up he puts a firm hand around her torso and begins to steer her inside.

"Let's get you dried off, Baroness," he says cheerfully. "And then perhaps we can discuss a new location for your wonderful consulting job. I don't think it's working out here."

I watch them go, smiling cattily when the baroness casts a glare back at me.

"Keep the straw in your pocket, sir," I say to myself.

"Ramya Knox."

I glance up and grin at Mrs. Burns. She's watching me with affection but also reproach. A smile that says, "You know what comes now."

"Is it detention, miss?" I ask sunnily. "Should I make it easier on myself and come quietly?"

"I think that would be best," Mrs. Burns says.

I follow her inside, grinning as the students cheer when I pass by them.

I'm still laughing as they dance in the cold jet of the awakened fountain.

CHAPTER TWENTY-THREE

FERRYMAN

Marley waits for me to finish detention. We leave the school building together, joking and laughing about the fact that the baroness left in a taxi after the whole incident, still soaking wet, and that she will not be returning. We reach the school gates and both stop in surprise.

An expensive car is waiting there.

"Could be a trap," Marley whispers, but I wave that comment away.

I can see who is in the backseat.

Her long silver hair is piled up and she is wearing a crisp afternoon dress, a blazer, and high heels with stockings. She opens the door and gestures for us to get in.

"Gran!" Marley exclaims.

"Here I was waiting for an hour like a fool," she says in her crisp Highland accent. "I'm not sure I need to ask which one of you had detention."

"It was Marley," I say. "He won't stop swearing."

Marley looks to Gran in terror, afraid she'll believe me, but she merely laughs once and then tells the chauffeur to drive.

"Where are we going?" I ask.

"We won't all fit into your mother's flat, Marley," Gran says loftily. "So we'll go to the Grassmarket."

The car stops outside Aunt Leanna's shop. Gran leads Marley and me to the back, where she slips open the door to the connecting tunnel, and the three of us descend into the now very familiar underground square.

"Keep up," Gran calls as we wind farther down the long corridor.

When we reach the market, it's relatively quiet, but I can see Mum, Opal, and Leanna all sitting in a booth. They've clearly been there for some time, and they all glance up in relief when we appear.

"Someone was put in detention," Gran says frankly as we join them in their booth, making it a party of six.

"Oh, Ramya," Mum says softly, while Opal smiles knowingly at me.

"I'm glad we can all be here to have this talk,"

Gran goes on. She reaches into her bag and pulls out a very small copper cup. She places it in the middle of the table.

Opal raises her hand but Gran holds up a finger and shakes her head. She turns to me instead, with an expectant look.

"What?" I ask, confused.

"Don't say 'what' to your grandmother," Mum says sharply.

"Oh, leave her, Cass," reprimands Opal, rolling her eyes.

"What do you want me to do with the cup?" I ask, frowning.

"Well," Gran says haughtily, "I'm thirsty."

I understand her meaning. I stare at the cup, concentrating. I hold my palm over it and try to connect and lock into that electric feeling I felt when falling from the bridge.

Water starts to pour from nowhere. No, not from nowhere—from me. It fills the cup and I quickly pull my hand away, to avoid it spilling over. I turn to Gran, then around the table, expecting everyone to be completely floored. Mum and her sisters smile at me, but Gran's face is blank.

"Good enough," she says swiftly. "But there is definite room for improvement."

My mouth drops open and I'm about to argue when I catch Mum's eye. I close my mouth, annoyed.

"You will spend your summer with me at the house," Gran announces grandly.

She calls her enormous country estate the house, which I find funny.

"And your aunt Opal will coach you."

Opal winks at me and I grin. But I can't ignore the quietly sad energy sitting next to me.

"I'll work all summer on witchcraft on one condition."

Gran raises an eyebrow in surprise. "Oh, yes?"

"Marley gets to come too."

Marley's face lights up at my words. Leanna makes a small, emotional noise, causing Mum to pat her gingerly on the arm. Gran watches me with something like reluctant pride.

"Of course."

I beam triumphantly.

Then the discussion ends, and my aunts and grandmother stand up. Marley follows, after a poke in the back from Gran. They move away from the booth, leaving me and Mum alone and sitting across from each other.

I watch her, still unforgiving. She stares just above my head. She flips her hand over, so the palm is facing the ceiling, and those same small flames dance on the surface of her skin.

I watch them, scenting the ash and feeling the fire. "Why didn't you tell me?"

She closes her palm, and the embers die. "Because I was scared you would be the same."

"The same as what?"

"As me."

"What happened to you?" I ask, instinctively knowing there are millions of molecules making up this person in front of me, someone I thought I understood completely.

"I'm the reason your aunt Opal was expelled."

I gape at her. "You?"

"Yes."

"How?"

"I was cornered by some bullies in the school toilets. I lost my temper. Set fire to half of a toilet stall. Your aunt came in and put it out. Then took the fall."

I can hardly believe it. "So you stopped magic completely?"

"I was too much fire for the world," she says calmly. "So I became ice."

"Grandpa knew."

"Of course. He wanted me to be like your aunt Opal. But our gifts are different."

I remember the frosty, unfeeling person she became that night. When Portia unleashed her power and turned family against family. Mum and Dad were so susceptible, and while Mum's temper has always been quick and pointed, she has become so cold. She's kept her own kind of Glamour up around herself, one that will never let in questions or deviations. I imagine those bursts of temper were the fire always trying to break free.

She then says something that stuns me. "Ramya, this family needs you. You are water. Water does not let the wind blow it in whichever direction it wishes. Water moves under its own laws. Just like you."

I look to the slick candlewick on the side of the table. Mum follows my gaze. She clicks her finger and a flame bursts into being. I let it sway for a moment before flicking my forefinger toward it.

A drop of water douses the flame, extinguishing it with a hiss. Mum wears a half smile that has sadness in its corners.

"We came here to get away from her," she finally says, an almost inaudible confession. "But she'll find us. In the end. And I hope, when she does, you'll be better than me."

I frown, unsure of what she means. Portia. Portia is the reason we came to Edinburgh?

"I did everything," Mum adds, getting to her feet, "in the hope you would be better than me." She straightens her clothes and moves strands of hair out of her face. "Now I need to speak with your grandmother. She's quite right. You need to be trained. This summer. And, Ramya?"

"Yes?"

"It will be hard. You might want to give up."

I meet her gaze. She's not being mean; she's asking if I'm really ready to do this. She maybe has not yet realized what I have discovered about myself during these last few years, with all the therapy and the handwriting workshops and the labeling and the othering and the noise.

I am resilience. I have a brain and a pair of hands and two eyes that do things differently than the rest of the herd. Where they see gray, I see silver. Where they see ponies, I see dark and deadly kelpies, who rise from the deep and bring your greatest fear with them. My hands may sometimes shake, but that won't stop them from reaching. My steps may cause me to fall more times than I would care to admit, but no one can get back up more quickly than I do.

If I have to fail one hundred times inside a world that was never designed for me, then so be it. It will make winning all the more glorious.

Magic is easy to me. Magic is just the art of letting all that resilience sing.

Later, I watch Mum and Gran have a quiet, private conversation. I watch Marley take Leanna for a tour around the market, showing her all the different vendors. Opal stands next to me.

"See that door in the far corner?"

I look to where she's pointing. It is yet another

entrance or exit in this market that seems to materialize only when spoken about. "Uh-huh?"

"I think there's someone on the other end who would like a word."

I stare up at her in bemusement, but she only smiles and walks away, disappearing into the market with her sister and nephew. I head over to the door, letting myself into an uphill corridor. It will inevitably be another tunnel leading to a shop front somewhere. I walk cautiously until I eventually reach a heavy door.

I knock.

I knock, again.

A grate on the door slides open and a pair of eyes look down at me.

"You're here!"

The door opens and I find myself walking into the very first bookshop I visited in Edinburgh.

Avizandum.

It's as dimly lit as ever. The Stranger is seated upon the front desk, reading something. He grins widely at me as I step inside.

"You did beautifully, Ramya."

I smirk. "No thanks to you."

He laughs. Then presents me with something. Something small and green.

"Grandpa's book!"

"I have sway with other booksellers," he says teasingly.

I hug it close to me. Then quickly put it in my bag before he can take it back. Once it's safe, I glance up at the Stranger. Trying to take in the details of his face, trying to remember him.

"The medusa hex," I say, pointing to the window facing out onto the row leading up to Greyfriars. "My aunt cast that spell, didn't she?"

He gleams. "The most powerful witch I know. Well. For now."

He regards me pointedly.

I shake my head. "Who are you? I mean, for real. Don't say a bookseller or a lawyer. Who are you?"

His smile doesn't fade. "I told you. I help people get their affairs in order."

"Then what's your name?"

The question is physically difficult to ask, as if proximity to him makes it more impossible.

"I've had so many names," he answers happily. "None of them really matter."

"I called out for help," I say. "That night I went to the island. I asked for help."

"You did."

"But you didn't come."

"I didn't need to."

"I could have died," I say cuttingly. "I didn't realize how much danger I was in until it was too late."

Not entirely true.

"Well," he says, a glint in his dark, quick eyes. "No one knows death until it is looking them in the face."

We stare at each other.

"All this magic . . ." I gesture around the room, but I really mean the city. Edinburgh. "Everything has changed. Glamour, witchcraft, the fae. Sirens. Is there . . . I mean, if I wanted to track someone down. Speak to someone who was maybe no longer here. Would that be possible? With all this magic, is that something I can do?"

His grin fades, all humor gone. Instead, he looks at me sadly. "No, Ramya. That is not possible."

I knew he would say that. I still needed to ask him.

"Ramya Knox." He says my name as if he's marveling at it. "I'll tell you one thing. He is so proud of you."

I feel something release in me. The broken arrow. It's fallen out, at last. I feel the tears flowing easily and unashamedly. I smile back and he places one hand on my shoulder, squeezing it gently.

"All right," I say, wiping my eyes and laughing. "I'd better get back."

"Yes," he agrees. "Give my love to the three witches."

I snort. "I will."

I head to the door, pulling it open and revealing the tunnel once more when—

"Oh, Ramya?"

I stop. I turn. "Yes?"

"I hear that you'll be spending your summer by Loch Ness?"

"Yes," I reply. "With Marley, Gran, and Opal. Learning about witchcraft."

"Very good. A beautiful part of the world. But you should know . . ."

"Yes?"

He grins at me. "They say there is a monster in the loch. Some kind of ancient beast. Few have been able to claim they have actually seen it, though. I wouldn't worry. Just myths and fairy tales, I would wager. Like trolls and fae and vampires."

I stare, agog. If he is telling me there really is a monster, and that it can simply glamour its way out of being caught . . .

His laughter still echoes throughout the bookshop as he disappears in front of me, leaving me alone.

I'm laughing too.

As I walk along the tunnel, back to the Grassmarket. Back to my family. All of us, together for the first time in my life. I feel a sense of freedom and optimism that I didn't know was possible. As if the newly claimed magic in me is carrying me along.

I'm not alone in the water. I'm not alone anywhere. I touch my bag, which holds two important books. One written for me and one written by me. I think of my cousin, now my best friend. I think of Mum and her fiery hands, to go with the temper I always knew was there. I think of Aunt Leanna and her cooking and her house full of nature. I think of Aunt Opal and our secret smile. The feeling of soaring across the Firth of Forth while kelpies leaped alongside us.

I think of Gran and her huge manor house. Where I will soon learn how to control magic.

I think of all the hundreds of species of Hidden Folk still out there for me to find. To learn from, to understand. To document. Portia is still out there. Many like her are, as well. I know this is only the beginning.

I take a turn among the tunnels and follow a cold draft of air. I follow the breeze to Greyfriars Kirk. I walk among the stone and let the cool caress my face, in a quiet oasis inside the bustling city.

As if it were planned, Marley is sitting in the exact same spot as the night I found him here.

"Hey?" I call.

He looks up, surprise turning to a smile.

"Want me to show you something?"

He nods enthusiastically at the question. "Always."

★

MARLEY AND I STARTED THIS adventure together, without the adults, and I need to show him what I've discovered.

We reach the edge of the water. Aunt Opal is watching from the front of Leanna's car, and her expression is stern. It says, "One false move and I'll be out of this car, and you'll be punished until the summer holidays."

I touch the water and I hear it sing.

When the kelpie appears, Marley stiffens. But he must remember. I can feel the moment he does. The same creature who once terrified him was also the one who carried him safely from the island. The kelpie moves closer, releasing all his Glamour so that Marley can witness his large and horrifying form.

Terrifyingly beautiful.

When he bows low, I tell Marley to climb up. When I don't follow, Marley frowns.

"What are you doing?" he asks.

If the kelpie were a regular horse, I would touch

his flank and signal for him to run. However, he is of course no normal horse. He starts to gallop without instruction, causing Marley to grab onto his seaweed mane with glee and terror.

I look back to Aunt Opal. She gives me one silent nod.

The river is like an enormous watery runway, where birds take off instead of airplanes. I bend my knees and puff out a determined breath, focusing on the large bridges ahead. The kelpie trots and canters and jumps, while Marley whoops in approval.

I shake out my hands. I stretch my neck muscles. I let go of every single bad behavioral therapist's words. The tics they made me suppress, the instincts they said I needed to relearn, I lean into all of them.

Then I run. Full force and full speed.

My feet cross the water as though it were concrete. I feel the water pushing up beneath my feet, working to keep me above the surface. I push down against their force and I'm suddenly airborne. The river acted as a launchpad, allowing me to go from running across the flat of the water to flying through the air.

Marley's mouth drops open as he watches, and the kelpie snorts, as if to say, "Show-off!"

I wave my hand toward the two of them and they are briefly splashed. Marley shrieks and the kelpie starts to chase me.

I scream with laughter.

No one can catch me. Not tonight.

I soar high enough to look out over the city. My city. This strange country that Grandpa loved so much. While people pretend it is this quaint and adorable place full of folk legends, I know the truth. I can see the centuries of stories for what they truly are. While tourists putter around above, I know who lives below.

And I'm a part of that.

I did it, Grandpa. I let myself drop, only to feel the water rise to hurtle me up once again. *I did what you wanted me to.* I drop again, fast. I let my feet dip beneath the top of the water, then project myself right back up. I suppose I never felt the full emptiness of his leaving because he is still here. Still etched into the lines of this land and its water. Still alive in the memories of the Hidden Folk who inhabit the corners and crevices.

Still alive in me.

I keep one hand pressed against the beret he gave me. I never want to lose it. It's what makes me feel like I can do this. Or rather it reminds me that I can.

A part of me thought I would get some kind of reward after this journey. Maybe a small fragment of me thought I would see him standing in front of me again.

But the reward is this feeling. Knowing that you

did a good thing for the right reasons. That you proved your enemies wrong.

I spent so much time tormenting myself about how I was going to go on without him, but I don't have to. Neither does Marley. We don't have to leave people behind because they've moved on to another part of their story, they can continue in ours.

Grandpa, I miss you. I miss the parts I didn't even get to know. I'm still working out how to tell this story without you but I'm going to do it. I'm not any of the things those people said. I'm like *you* said. You were right all along. I won't doubt it again.

I think of my community here. A shield against those who seek chaos and division. The one you helped me to build, even from beyond.

I smile. I feel light. I feel free. I feel ready.

I wave my beret in the breeze of the river and hold it up to the sky. I may not remember the Stranger's face, but I remember his words.

He is so proud of you.

I feel beloved and stylish all at once.

Glamourous.

The End. Ish.

ACKNOWLEDGMENTS

I have to start by thanking the readers, because they erase all the bad and replace it with unknowable good. Thank you to everyone who has given Addie, Cora, and now Ramya a place on their shelves.

Thank you to Lauren, the kindest and most capable.

Thank you to the booksellers again and again until I die. A bunch of lockdown books, and you still found a place for them. Thank you to Gav, Helen, Clara, and all of the wonderful people who have sold my stories. This book is entirely about bookshops and the wonder they hold. Thank you for all of it.

Thank you to Waterstones, Blue Peter, and Blackwell's for changing my life.

Thank you to the bloggers and reviewers. Thank you for the Chapter Thirteen memes.

Thank you to Eishar. McDonald's in the back of

the Uber and meetings in the coffee shop. But thank you for taking on Ramya and her slightly chaotic world. Thank you for not making me write the same book over and over again. You're a supernova of an editor.

Thank you to Aimée and the whole Knights Of team. You keep standards so high.

Thank you to Ella for your brilliant marketing brain, Thy and Tia for your wonderful design work, and Viki for proofreading, the thankless but essential part of the process!

Thank you to Jennifer Bell for taking a fragile and frightened new lockdown author out to lunch.

Thank you to Ross Montgomery, Frank Cottrell-Boyce, Sharna Jackson, Maz Evans, Jen Campbell, Lizzie Huxley-Jones, Anna James, Patience Agbabi, Malorie Blackman, Robin Stevens, and Alastair Chisholm for being just generally lovely in a not-so-lovely time. Katherine Rundell, too. You came up to me at a launch party, said very kind things, and then told funny and self-deprecating stories about your school visits. It was a generous and classy thing to do for someone like me, who knew very few people and is constantly afraid.

Thank you to the Rights team for championing my books across borders.

Thank you to Annabelle at EDPR. If I ever thank

a higher power in a speech, just know that I mean you.

Thank you to Danielle and CJ for a hilarious day running around London bookshops, and thank you to Bounce for your bolstering and cheerleading.

Thank you to Kay and Marssaié. I wish you were with me in schools when the readers tell me how much they love your covers. Almost as much as me.

Thank you to the 9 Story team for, well, you know.

Thank you to Josh for always listening to the first read-through.

Thank you to my extended family for being supportive and buying the books.

Thank you to Mum for keeping me humble.

Thank you to Dad. Still my best friend, three books on.

And to my grandpa. Who, in his own way, helped to save the world.

ABOUT THE AUTHOR

Elle McNicoll is a bestselling and award-winning novelist. Her debut, *A Kind of Spark,* is a Schneider Family Book Award honor title, a Blue Peter Book Awards Best Story winner, the overall winner of the Waterstones Children's Book Prize in 2021, and Blackwell's Book of the Year for 2020. She has been nominated for the Carnegie Medal and was short-listed for the Books Are My Bag Readers Awards, the Branford Boase Award, and the Little Rebels Children's Book Award. Her second novel, *Show Us Who You Are,* was a Blackwell's Book of the Month title and one of the *Bookseller*'s Best Books of the Year. She is an advocate for better representation of neurodiversity in publishing and currently lives in East London.

ellemcnicoll.com